THE FLOODS

1

Neighbours

Colin Thompson

illustrations by the author

RANDOM HOUSE AUSTRALIA

This work is fictitious. Any resemblance to anyone living or dead is purely coincidental.

A Random House book
Published by Random House Australia Pty Ltd
Level 3, 100 Pacific Highway, North Sydney, NSW 2060
www.randomhouse.com.au

Floods 1: Neighbours first published by Random House Australia in 2005
Floods 2: Playschool first published by Random House Australia in 2006
This bindup edition first published in 2008

Addresses for companies within the Random House Group can be found at www.randomhouse.com.au/offices.

Thompson, Colin (Colin Edward)
The Floods 1 & 2 bindup.

ISBN 978 1 74166 305 1 (pbk.)

Series: Thompson, Colin (Colin Edward). The Floods; 1 & 2
For primary school age.

Witches – Juvenile fiction.
Wizards – Juvenile fiction.
Family – Juvenile fiction.

A823.3

Design, illustrations and typesetting by Colin Thompson
Additional typesetting by Anna Warren, Warren Ventures
Printed and bound by Griffin Press, South Australia

Random House Australia uses papers that are natural, renewable and recyclable products and made from wood grown in sustainable forests. The logging and manufacturing processes are expected to conform to the environmental regulations of the country of origin.

10 9 8 7 6 5 4 3 2 1

The Floods' Family Tree

MERLIN ♥ **MORDONNA**
Wizard   Witch

Valla
Boy - 22

Satanella
Girl - 16

Merlinmary
Not sure - 15

Winchflat
Boy - 14

Morbid & Silent
Twin boys - 11

Betty
Girl - 10

The Floods

Turn to page 144 for The Flood Family Files.

Normal people

Turn down ANY street to see them.

Here
Lies
CHAPTER
1

At first glance, as long as you are at least a hundred metres away and see them from the back on a dark autumn evening when it's raining, the Floods look like any other family. There is a mum and a dad and some children. They all have two eyes, one head, two arms and two legs and hair on top of their heads – except Satanella, who has no arms but four legs and hair all over her body.

At second glance, especially if you're *less* than a hundred metres away and see them from the front, the Floods do not look like any other family. Mum and Dad and most of the children always wear black clothes. Even Satanella wears a black collar encrusted with black diamonds against her black fur. Only the

youngest, Betty, is different. Her hair is blonde and she wears ordinary, brightly coloured clothes and skips a lot.

The Floods are a family of witches and wizards, even Betty, although she looks almost normal. She likes looking different from the rest of them. It makes her feel special. It also lulls the world into a false sense of security. She is the only one of the Floods who people don't cross the road to avoid.

They even feel sorry for her and say, 'Look at that sweet little girl having to live with those weird people, poor thing.'

It all started when Betty's mother, Mordonna, decided that six children who were witches or wizards was enough. Valla, Satanella, Merlinmary, Winchflat and the twins, Morbid and Silent, were each, in their own weird and scary way, the sort of children any witch or wizard parent would be very proud of.

Satanella, for example, is not the family pet – she's actually one of the children, but because of an unfortunate accident with a prawn and a faulty wand, she was turned into a fox terrier. Although

it's possible to reverse the spell, Satanella has actually grown to like being on all fours. Merlinmary also has hair all over her body[1] but she is not a dog, even though she does growl a lot and likes chasing sticks.

'I would like a little girl,' Mordonna said to her husband, Nerlin, after the twins were born. 'A pretty little girl who wants to dress up dolls in nice frocks instead of turning them into frogs. I want a little girl who I can do cooking with and make cakes that taste like chocolate instead of bat's blood.'

'But, sweetheart, we're wizards and witches,' said Nerlin. 'Turning things into frogs and blood is what we do. Our families have done it since the dawn of time.'

'I know, and I adore frogs and blood,' said Mordonna, 'and I love our six wonderfully talented, evil children who are as vile as your wildest dreams.

---

[1] *No one is sure if Merlinmary is he or she because he or she is so hairy that no one can get near enough to find out. Throughout this book Merlinmary will be referred to as 'she' but please remember she might be he or something weird that isn't either.*

I just want one pretty little girl to do ordinary mummy and daughter things with.'

'But you grow death-cap mushrooms with the twins and you sharpen the cat's teeth with Valla.'

'Yes, yes, I know,' Mordonna replied, 'and I love all those things, but what about knitting and painting pictures of flowers?'

'What's knitting?' said Nerlin, but Mordonna had made up her mind. She was going to have one more child and that child would be a normal, ordinary girl with no magical powers. And instead of being made in a laboratory using an ancient recipe book, a very big turbocharged wand and a set of shiny Jamie Oliver saucepans, like some of the other children had been, this new child would be made the same way as you and I were.[2]

When Betty was born, she looked just like the pretty little girl Mordonna had dreamt of. Of course, being a wizard's child she was very advanced for her age, and by the time she was three she was helping

---

[2] *Well, I was. I can't say how you were made. You could have been knitted for all I know.*

her mum make soufflés and had knitted a cardigan for her granny, Queen
Scratchrot. (The queen, with several
other friends and relations, is buried in
the back garden
and feels the
cold on winter
nights because
most of her skin
has rotted away.)

But no matter how
'normal' she looks, Betty
still has magic inside her.
It's just little things
most people wouldn't
notice – like when she
reaches for a book way
above her head and
suddenly the
book is there
on the table.
Or when a glass floats across the kitchen, fills itself

up at the tap, the water turning into cordial with two ice cubes and a straw, and then floats back into Betty's left hand.

Here
Lies
CHAPTER
2

Where the Floods live is a bit like them. From a distance it looks ordinary, but up close, it isn't. They don't live in a big dark menacing castle in Transylvania Waters like all their other relations. They live in a normal country in a normal city[3] in an ordinary street in a house with a front garden and a back garden. Except the Floods' house is kind of different.

It isn't because the hedge tries to reach out and

---

[3] *My editor asked me to name the town where the Floods live, but I won't, because you might feel safe and secure knowing they don't live near you – and we wouldn't want that, would we? And if you* do *live in their town, you might start bothering them and get yourself turned into a toad, and then your parents might sue me, unless being a toad was an improvement on what you are now.*

touch you when you walk by, and it isn't because the garden is so overgrown you can't see the house. It isn't because there are three black clouds always hovering over it, even on a bright sunny day, or that huge black vampire bats hang in every tree. And it certainly isn't because the Floods are nasty to everyone. They aren't. If people weren't too scared to ask, the Floods would happily lend them their lawnmower (if they had one) or give them a cup of sugar.

When the Floods bought the house, it was the same as all the others in the street. It had a neat lawn at the front and back with beds of pretty flowers. The front door was red and the windows had bright white awnings and shiny clean glass.

The only thing the Floods didn't change was the front door.

'A lovely shade of fresh blood,' Mordonna had said, 'but the rest will have to go.'

They painted the window awnings black and added cobwebs and dead flies. They pulled up all the awful flowers and planted thistles and stinging nettles and made it quite clear to the lawn that if

it didn't stop growing, it was concrete time. They buried their various dead and semi-dead friends and relations in the back garden and trained the front gate to keep out unwanted visitors.

People usually cross the road rather than walk by the gate. The mailman puts the letters in the box with a long pair of barbecue tongs ever since the day the mailbox ate his watch.

Underneath the house, the Floods created a vast maze of cellars and tunnels that reach out in all directions for hundreds of metres. The lowest level is so deep underground, you can feel the heat from the centre of the Earth and actually fry an egg on the floor.

And around the edge of the garden, they planted a tall, thick, vicious hedge that keeps out most prying eyes, though not all, as we shall see later.

The Floods are a happy, loving family and they think their house is perfect. The problem is everyone else. Most people don't like things to be different. They want everyone to have the same things they've got – the same car, the same wide-screen television, the same barbecue and the same two-point-four children. Then they can go to the supermarket and all feel the same, and all talk about the TV programme they watched last night and where they're all going on their holidays.

In fact, it's not quite that simple. Secretly most people want to be exactly the same as everyone else – only a bit better. They want their car to be the one with the luxury bits and bigger engine and they want their children to be better at school, and they want to have more money and a spa bath that all their neighbours haven't got.

So really, everyone is jealous of everyone else.

Except the Floods.

They don't even have a car. If they want to go anywhere they either travel by turbo broomsticks that go so fast ordinary people can't see them,[4] or else they walk or take a taxi. Apart from Betty, they never go on the bus because people complain about the smell – which isn't so much bad as weird, like roses mixed with pepper and wet dog. And if they want a spa bath, they take off their clothes and stand in the back garden while their three black clouds rain on them. Not cold rain like you and I would get, but warm rain that even has shampoo and conditioner in it. Until recently they didn't even have a television.

So while everyone in the street thinks the Floods are strange, scary and different and never invite them to their coffee mornings or Tupperware parties, the Floods are probably happier than all of them. Apart from the eldest son, Valla, they don't even go out

---

[4] *You know how sometimes you think you see something out of the corner of your eye and when you turn around there's nothing there? Well, that's one of the Floods going by. Even if you had eyes in the back of your head and didn't blink, you still wouldn't be able to see them because they travel faster than the speed of light.*

to work, because they have everything they need without having to.

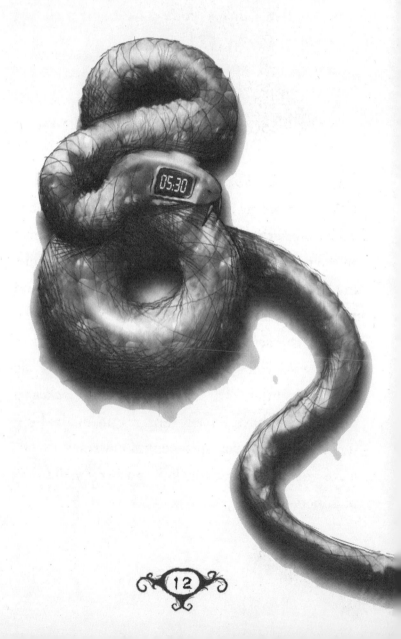

Monday morning, 5.30 am

As the morning light peeped in through the blood-red curtains, the Floods' alarm snake bit Mordonna on the neck and woke her up. An alarm snake is like an alarm clock except it doesn't make any noise and it wakes you up by biting you on the neck. (Which means it isn't actually like an alarm clock at all, except it does wake you up and it does alarm you.) The big advantage of the alarm snake is that it only wakes up the person it bites, so someone else in the bed can stay fast asleep. If you are a normal human, it doesn't wake you up so much as kill you because it's very poisonous.

Nerlin was lying on his back with his mouth open, snoring like a hippopotamus that had just swallowed a rusty steam train. The alarm snake licked the sleep from Mordonna's eyes and slithered into the next room to wake Valla. Mordonna checked herself in the mirror to see that she was still as beautiful as she had been when she went to bed, and then went downstairs to start the day.

'Come on, everyone,' she shouted as she went downstairs. 'Time to get up, time to get ready for school.'

There were seven children and only one bathroom, so there were the usual fights over who got in first, just like in normal houses. Everyone tried to get there before Merlinmary because it could take her up to an hour to do her hair, on account of the fact that it covers every square centimetre of her body. She even has hair on her eyeballs and tongue. While she was in the bathroom, though, she charged up all the electric razors and toothbrushes.

Breakfast in the Flood house was probably a bit different from your house. Vlad the cat hung around under the kitchen table rubbing against someone's leg. No one ever discovered where the leg had come from or who it belonged to, but it was there every morning.

There was a lot more running around than in normal houses. Not because the children were out of control, but because their breakfasts kept trying to get away from them.

'Morbid, Silent, would you stop juggling your breakfast and just eat it,' snapped Mordonna.

'Yeah, but look, Mum – we can make it stick to the ceiling,' said Morbid. Silent simply nodded vigorously and grunted. He always thinks exactly the same as his twin and can't see the point in just repeating everything Morbid says.

'Anyone can make slugs stick to the ceiling, dear. Just eat them up while they're still nice and slimy.'

Of course, there was always at least one slug that slid out of the bread and vanished under the stove.

'Betty, stop teasing the sugar bats,' said Mordonna. 'Just put them in the warm milk and eat them up, or you'll have to go back to baby food.'

The trouble was that Betty wasn't really old enough for sugar bats. She was only ten and her hands were too small to control them. She didn't actually tease them – that would be cruel – but every time she got one on her spoon and held it up to her mouth, it tried to fly off and hide behind the fridge. In the end she had to eat them with her fingers, even though it wasn't a very well-behaved thing to do.

Vlad, the cat, added to the general chaos by leaping about on the kitchen units trying to catch the bats, which of course he never did.

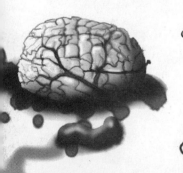

After breakfast Vlad always felt depressed for an hour or so. He had no problem ripping little birds to bits, but he had

never once caught a bat. No one had thought to tell him that sugar bats have radar and could see him coming.

Winchflat and Merlinmary didn't do much better. Their rats' brains were so slippery they kept falling on the floor and slithering off to join the slugs under the stove.

'Oh, for goodness' sake, children, if you can't stop mucking about, I'm just going to make you eat cornflakes,' said Mordonna, tipping Satanella's accountant's entrails into her bowl by the back door. Satanella always had her meals right next to the cat-flap so she could make a quick exit into the garden. Quite often she had to throw her food up and eat it again several times before she could finally keep it down.

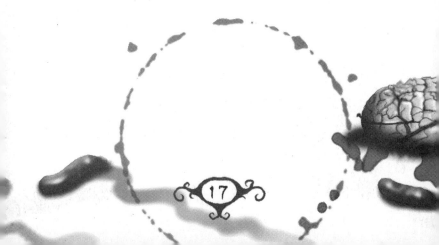

'Yeuuuwww, cornflakes,' said Morbid.

'Gross,' said Betty.

By the time the six youngest children had caught their breakfast and either eaten it or sucked its insides out, there was barely time to wipe the blood and slime off their chins[5] before the wizard school bus materialised in one of the cellars.

'Come on, kids, hurry up. The bus will be here in a minute,' Mordonna told them all. 'Tangle your hair and do make sure you've got blood under every single one of your fingernails. I don't want the other parents thinking I don't bring you up properly.'

'Mum, Satanella's eaten my homework,' said Merlinmary.

'Well, she'll just have to bring it up again when you get to school,' her mother replied. 'And Morbid, do remember to lock your school bag. I don't want your lunch crawling out and biting the bus driver again.'

---

[5] *And wring out the sponge into a bowl for the night eels' breakfast. (See the back of the book for information about the night eels and other Flood family pets.)*

(There are two reasons the bus appears in the cellar. Firstly, that's where the bus stop is; and secondly, the bus that takes five of the children to school is not an ordinary bus, so if it did appear in the street outside the Floods' house, it would scare the living daylights out of the neighbours.

The school is a special wizard and witch school, hidden away from the normal world in a secret valley right up in the mountains in darkest Patagonia. To reach the school each day, Satanella, Merlinmary, Winchflat and the twins have to cross several oceans, some of which can get very angry. They also travel over a desert or two, through fifty-metre snowdrifts, up a tall waterfall and across a bottomless lake. All of which, of course, an ordinary bus would find a bit difficult to do. In fact, an ordinary bus wouldn't get more than twenty metres across the sea before sinking.

The wizard school bus, on the other hand, covers all these vast distances in nine minutes. To call the wizard bus a bus is stretching the definition of the word 'bus'. The wizard bus is not so much a bus as a dragon with seats and a toilet.)

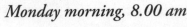

Monday morning, 8.00 am

At last the Floods' house grew quiet again. Mordonna checked herself in the mirror.

'Still staggeringly beautiful,' she said and sat down with a huge cup of strong coffee.

The remaining Flood child, Valla, finally came downstairs. He had the good sense to stay in bed cuddling his pet vampire bats, Nigel and Shirley, until the other kids were out of the house. Then he got up and spent a relaxed ten minutes in the bathroom bleaching his face, before going downstairs for a quick cup of milkman's blood.[6] He would then take the unknown leg from under the kitchen table and give it to Nigel and Shirley to chew on while he was at work.

Valla was the manager of the local blood-bank. To him, his job was like he died and went to heaven.

---

[6] *Valla believed that because milkmen always get up very early, if he drank some milkman's blood for breakfast it would wake him up and get his day off to a bright start.*

He loved his work so much that he often took it home with him. Both his bedroom and his underground playroom were littered with bags of blood, labelled and catalogued like fine wines. His favourite blood was the rare type OOH+, which came from only one person in the whole world – a beautiful Australian singer with a very famous bottom. Valla had just one small bag of her blood, which he drank one drop at a time and only on very special occasions. To cover up the fact that he was taking more blood out of the blood-bank than people were putting in, he replaced it with fake blood made out of tomato sauce, frog's spit and a rare plant root from Tristan da Cuhna. Most of the time this worked fine and patients receiving Valla's fake blood hardly ever turned hyperactive or dropped dead.

GREAT-UNCLE BLADDER

Monday morning, 8.30 am

Peace had descended briefly on the house. The alarm snake, having recovered from the headache it always got after biting Valla, slithered back into the parents' bedroom to wake up Nerlin, who had just come to the best bit of his dream.[7]

'Morning, handsome,' said Mordonna as her husband stumbled into the kitchen. 'How are we feeling today? Good night's sleep?'

'Mmmm,' Nerlin mumbled. 'My mouth tastes like a very old washing machine full of dirty socks.'

'That's nice, dear. Want some coffee?'

'In a minute. I'm still enjoying the socks.'

'Good dreams?'

'Oh yes,' said Nerlin. 'My favourite.'

'Oh, the one with the, err …?'

'Yes.'

'And the big pink …?'

'That's the one,' said Nerlin. 'I just love that dream and, you know, it never gets boring.'

---

[7] *Which my editor said I'm not allowed to tell you about. So I'm afraid you'll just have to make up Nerlin's dream yourself.*

'Well, it wouldn't, would it?' said Mordonna. 'Was I wearing the shiny thing?'

'Absolutely. Think I better have that coffee now.'

The peace didn't last long. A few minutes later the thump, thump, thump of disco music mixed with shouting and swearing drifted over from the house next door. Then the neighbours' dog started barking, a big thundering bark that made the cups rattle.

You know how when everything seems perfect and you think life just couldn't get any better, something always spoils it? This was the something that did that to the Floods.

The neighbours from hell – the Dents.

'Mmm, not even nine o'clock. They're starting early today,' said Mordonna, getting up from her chair.

'Yes,' Nerlin agreed. 'We'll have to do something about it. It's really getting on my nerves.'

'No point in phoning the police. They never do anything.'

'No, no, we'll sort it out ourselves.'

'Well, I'm off to do the housework,' said Mordonna. 'See that the spiders are working properly.'

'Yes, I'll do the mould and then do the pets. I suppose it's pointless me asking if the kids fed them?'

'As if.'

With the Dents' noise echoing through the house, Mordonna went from room to room checking for cobwebs. Where there weren't any, she left fresh spiders with detailed weaving patterns and, to encourage them, she put a few juicy bluebottles in with them.

Nerlin went down into the cellars to check the damp and spray the walls with a hose to make sure the mould stayed nice and healthy. Down on the third level, he could still hear the Dents – a muffled blur of bangs and crashes. Then he fed the cellar pets: the night eels, the giant hipposlugs and Doris, the seven-hundred-year-old blind dodo. Of course, like most families, the pets belonged to the children, who always forgot to look after them, so their parents had to. Cleaning out the litter tray of a seven-hundred-year-old blind dodo was not a job for the faint-hearted or anyone with a good sense of smell. By the time Nerlin had staggered outside and tipped the contents over the vegie garden he felt pretty faint and had to sit on Mordonna's mother's grave and breathe deeply for a few minutes.[8]

'Morning, mother-in-law. How are the maggots wriggling?' he asked, and the mound of earth beneath him shivered in reply as Queen Scratchrot twitched her bones.

'Oh well, better get on,' said Nerlin.

After the cobwebs, Mordonna went back through every room checking the dust was properly organised – not too thick on the table tops and nicely gathered into hairy piles in the corners. By the time she'd done that, the kitchen frogs had clambered over the dirty dishes and licked them clean; the crusty toad had nibbled all the hard burnt bits off the pans and the cutlery snake had slithered his tongue between

---

[8] *It has to be said, though, that where Nerlin emptied Doris's litter tray, the lettuces grew two metres tall.*

every prong of every fork. All Mordonna had to do was put everything back in the cupboards.

The noise from next door always faded a bit after lunch. That was when Mr Dent, after a hard morning shouting and swearing and a thick greasy lunch, fell asleep and Mrs Dent settled down to watch an American reality show full of people that made even her look good.

Nerlin and Mordonna took advantage of the temporary peace by having an afternoon sleep, doing a bit of gardening and trimming Grandma's toenails where they grew out of her grave by the clothesline. Then it was teatime, followed by another short snooze before the kids came home from school.

If it hadn't been for the wretched Dents next door, life would have been perfect.

Here
Lies
CHAPTER
4

When the Floods moved into number 13 Acacia Avenue, there had been two nice old couples in the houses on either side. Life had been peaceful. Their neighbours had brought them cake, and in return the Floods had given them crispy fried cockroaches. One of the advantages of having old people for neighbours is that they often can't see very well, so when the Flood children gave them bowls of crispy fried cockroaches – which are delicious, by the way – they thought they were bits of crispy bacon.

The disadvantage of having old people for neighbours is that they die a lot. Even after Winchflat, who was the scientific brains of the Flood family, had used his Massive-Electric-Shock-Dead-Person-

iReviver[9] on the old couple at number 11, they only came back to life for a few weeks.

That was when the Dents moved in and shattered the calm of the whole street.

They were the neighbours from hell. Not real hell where some of the Floods' best friends lived, but hell-on-Earth – which isn't actually a real place, more a state of mind. If you think of the worst person you've ever met or seen on TV, the Dents were much worse than that.

The Dents fought each other and swore a lot in very loud voices. They filled their front yard with rusty old cars and broken machines and their back yard with thousands of empty bottles and other garbage, which often ended up in the Floods' garden. In one of the old cars out the front, they kept a ferocious dog called Rambo that tried to bite everyone.

All their clothes were made of shiny nylon and Mr Dent had a terrible moustache and a big gold chain. Mrs Dent had lumpy legs you could see

---

[9]   *See page 156 for instructions on how to build your own.*

way too much of and her hair looked like cushion stuffing that had been soaking in a bucket of bleach. Mr Dent's job was making sure he never had a job – which there wasn't much chance of anyway. When he was eighteen he had been sent to work cleaning out the pipes at the sewerage works, but they sacked him after two days because the pipes were more disgusting after he'd been inside them than they had been before. That had taken a lot of sneaky skill on his part, but to make extra sure he was never given a job again, he slipped in the sludge and hurt his back just enough to get a pension.

Mrs Dent's job was avoiding Mr Dent and anything that kept her away from the TV.

They had two vile children: Tracylene, who had way too many boyfriends, way too much eye-liner and way too few brain cells, and Dickie, who was ten, but should never have been allowed to become one, never mind two, three, four, etc. Dickie's hobby was breaking into other people's houses, peeing on their furniture and putting Barbie dolls in their microwaves.

Dickie was in the same class as Betty Flood and, when he wasn't stealing other kids' dinner money, he used to sit behind her and pull her hair and call her names.

The only Flood child who didn't go to the wizard school was Betty. To try to make her less wizardy, Mordonna sent Betty to the normal school a few streets away. Betty would have preferred to go to the same school as her brothers

and sisters. Normal people, if you could call Dickie Dent and all the other dumb kids in her class 'normal', were so dull and boring and stupid and ugly. None of them could see in the dark or even make a pencil move without using their hands, or in Dickie's case, his nose.

When she had started school, Betty decided that no matter how many lessons her parents made her take, she would stay different. Not that she had any choice in the matter. Boring facts went in her left ear and rushed out of the right one as quickly as they could. Betty couldn't even learn her nine times table. This was not because she was stupid, but because Betty knew that these things aren't important.

'You're a witch, you are,' Dickie hissed at Betty when the teacher wasn't looking.

'You needn't think that saying nice things like that is going to make me like you,' said Betty, and she made six huge pimples swell up on his forehead.

'Miss, Miss,' Dickie cried, 'she's made me come out in spots.'

'Dickie Dent, don't be such a stupid little boy,' said the teacher. 'People can't give you spots.'

Betty put on her best sweet little girl face, which always made the teacher want to cuddle her. Then she made Dickie's six spots burst and run down his face.

'Miss, Miss, look what she done,' Dickie cried.

The teacher got so angry she made Dickie stay in during break and she wrote an angry letter to his parents – which was a waste of time really, because neither of them could read.

Betty would probably have stood out less if she had eaten ordinary school dinners instead of pickled lizards and toads' knees. She did try eating the school meat pies and turkey twizzlers once, but it only made her throw up.

'You're weird, you,' the other kids said to her, but Betty thought that was a compliment.

'Why's that, then?' said Betty, looking all innocent. She knew she was ten times brighter than any of the other kids would ever be and that she could get them every single time.

'Eating lizards and frogs, that's gross, that is,' they said.

'See your burgers?'

'Yeah?'

'This is what they're made of,' said Betty, and a huge smelly pile of gross animal bits appeared on the table. 'Look: cows' bottoms and eyelids, sheep's nostrils and chicken beaks and chemicals and scum.'

Then the children all felt that retching thing in their throats where you try really hard not to throw up, but know that nothing will stop it – and they did, all over the floor.

'Oh, look,' said Betty. 'Your sick looks *exactly* like your lunch.'

Which made the kids throw up again.

'You are all so dumb,' said Betty, and for good measure gave every child three big uncomfortable angry purple pimples on their bottoms, so no matter

how they sat down, it hurt. She gave Dickie an extra couple just to keep him on his toes – which of course it did, because it hurt too much to sit down.

'See,' she added. 'All that dreadful food gives you spots too.'

Here
Lies
CHAPTER
5

Lots of people hate their jobs. It's a part of their lives that is necessary to make money to buy food and houses and clothes. While they're at work they dream of the time when they won't be at work, when they'll be with their loved ones having a life. They dream of their hobbies, which are often like work, except people enjoy them.

Some lucky people actually enjoy their jobs – or to put it another way, some people actually love what they do all day. Mrs Dent loved being hypnotised by TV. She had a TV at the foot of the bed that she turned on as soon as she woke up. She had a waterproof TV in the shower and a tiny TV to look at as she went downstairs. Mr Dent loved what

he did all day, which was nothing plus eating plus drinking plus sleeping. Mr and Mrs Dent were even happy screaming at each other, which they did every day. As for the Floods, they would have been happy all of the time if it wasn't for the Dents.

Like most families, the Floods had hobbies that they loved. Under their house in the vast network of cellars, each Flood had a few rooms of their own where they could play or experiment to their heart's content. When the Floods were doing  their favourite things, and even on the rare occasions when there was not much noise coming from the Dents' house, the Dents were still there, niggling away at the back of everyone's mind. Even when the family was down in the deepest cellars, seven floors below the house, the Dents managed to spoil things.

Winchflat, the family genius, had a whole floor of cellars jam-packed with incredible equipment where he invented things that normal people would have shouted about and got very rich as a result of. Winchflat made a tiny pill that you put into water that would make a car go. He hadn't bothered to tell anyone about it because he always knew he could invent something better – like the car he was working on that could hover just above the ground, read your mind and take you to wherever you wanted to go, and not actually need the water with the pill in it to make it work because it was all powered by one single bumblebee and a dandelion. If it hadn't been for the endless drone of Mrs Dent's TV in the background, he would have had the whole thing finished. But that niggling noise just took the edge off his concentration.

In another cellar Merlinmary was

charging the batteries. Her hair was so full of electricity that at night she had to sleep in a lead-lined room with her fingers pushed into a special socket that charged up a huge bank of batteries, enough to run the whole house. She was born with this talent because the night Nerlin made her in the laboratory down in his cellar, using a recipe he hadn't tried before, there was a terrible storm like you get in the Frankenstein movies. The difference was that Nerlin did not need a bolt of lightning to bring Merlinmary to life, he only needed a teaspoon of Vegemite. So when the lightning had hit the house that night fifteen years before, racing down into the cellars and up the legs of the laboratory bench[10] at the very moment Nerlin was bringing Merlinmary to life, it filled the child with enough electricity to run the whole of America for seventy-five years.[11]

---

[10] *The lightning also ran up Nerlin's legs, but he quite liked that.*

[11] *This calculation is based on only 36.72% of the population using electric toothbrushes – so it could be a few years more or less.*

In fact Merlinmary had so much electricity inside her that she made the meter run backwards – which meant that every time the Floods got a power bill, the electricity company had to give them money.

Because of the distraction of Mr Dent revving up his clapped-out motorbikes, Merlinmary sometimes lost concentration and put her fingers in the socket back to front. This used to make her hair all frizzy and sometimes give half the town a power cut. With the Dents getting louder and louder, this was happening more and more.

Morbid and Silent bred beautiful moths in one of their rooms. They fed the baby caterpillars on the finest orchid petals and tucked their chrysalises up in tiny beds of cotton wool. They helped the baby moths emerge safely into the world and then pulled their wings off and ate them. (The wings, that is, not the moths – that would be disgusting.) Sometimes the Dents would start a shouting match and the twins would throw away the wings and eat the moths, which made them very sick.

Betty spent many happy hours making false wings for all the damaged moths that kept crawling under her door. She made them by boiling up cockroaches, spreading the sticky liquid out on a sheet of glass and cutting it into little wings.

When Mrs Dent threw saucepans around, Betty would lose her place and forget how many times she had wound up the rubber band to make the wings work, and the moths would snap in half.

Valla, even though he was obsessed with blood – so much so that he often took his own blood out to look at it under a microscope – had a soft spot for cockroaches and had a cellar with a tiny orphanage for all the baby cockroaches who had lost their parents in Betty's saucepan. His favourite bit was trying to give the cockroaches blood transfusions, which required complete silence and very great concentration. Once again the noise from the Dents' house distracted him and a lot of cockroaches exploded.

Winchflat loved the stars and planets and spent hours looking at them, which was very difficult from a cellar seven floors below ground. Instead of doing

the obvious thing like you or I would – which is to go outside or up on the roof – Winchflat got around the problem by actually bringing the stars down to him. He invented a fantastically powerful space vacuum cleaner that could suck whole galaxies out of the sky and into a bottle on his bench. He was a well brought up, tidy child so, naturally, when he'd finished looking at the galaxies, he always put them back. Always, that is, except Sunday, when a sudden explosion from the Dents' back yard – Dickie was playing with matches in the shed after eating three tins of baked beans – made Winchflat press button B *before* button A. The result was that a galaxy that should have been in the Milky Way was now on the opposite side of space, and it was upside down too.

Even Satanella had a cellar. In the middle of the floor there was a tree. First she would go and sniff it, then she would chase a cat up it. This was not Vlad, of course, but a special cat from Rent-A-Scaredy-Cat. Satanella then sat by the door waiting for the cat to try to escape – which it always did when Satanella got distracted by a sudden noise such as

the sound of Dickie Dent exploding again.

Mordonna kept offering to turn Satanella back into a little girl, but Satanella always refused, saying, 'Life is so simple when you're a dog. Eat, sleep, chase cats. That's it. Oh, and a bit of a tickle behind the ear, and of course stick and ball chasing. It doesn't get any better than that.' Although there were times she wished she was a girl again, so she could go and thump Dickie.

Winchflat made his little sister a Stick-And-Red-Rubber-Ball-Throwing Machine, which she kept in a very long narrow dungeon. No one else would admit it, but every single one of her brothers and sisters and her parents had played with the machine when they thought no one else was looking.[12] It was one of those family secrets that everyone else knew about but all pretended they didn't. I suppose it proves that it's true when people say, 'There is a bit of dog in all of us.'[13]

---

[12] *Winchflat made himself a Beep-Loudly-When-Anyone-Else-Is-Coming Machine so he would NEVER get caught chasing red rubber balls.*

[13] *Editor: 'No one says that.'*

43

Nerlin and Mordonna shared a cellar, but you're not old enough to know what it's for. Orange jelly, chains, socks, mugs of hot chocolate and a big armchair were involved (though not necessarily in that order), but even their hobby was spoilt by the Dents' noise.

Sunday afternoon, 3.42 pm – family meeting

'Something has to be done,' said Nerlin. 'Something permanent.'

'Yeah,' said Satanella. She liked the sound of 'permanent'. It made her think there might be a lot of blood involved.

'You can see why their name is Dent,' said Valla. 'They are a dent on the face of humanity.'

'Yeah,' everyone agreed.

'And what do you do to dents?' Betty asked.

'You fill them in,' said Winchflat.

'But not before you've bashed them as flat as you can first,' said Morbid. Silent nodded.

'Grrrr,' said Satanella, thinking how nice it would be to chew on a Dent leg bone.

'Couldn't we just put a "be nice" spell on them?' said Mordonna.

'That's boring,' said Betty. 'Anyway, they're ugly and stupid and we want them out of our street.'

'Actually, we want them out of our town,' said Winchflat.

'Galaxy,' said Valla.

'I think you should go and talk to them, before we do anything,' said Mordonna.

'Okay, my darling, but it won't do any good,' said Nerlin. 'You can't reason with people like that.'

'I'll come with you, Dad,' offered Merlinmary. 'If there's any trouble, I can give them an electric shock.'

The Dents had turned their front yard into a pigsty, except no decent pig would ever have wanted to live there. There were three rusty old cars – one where Rambo the dog lived, another where Tracylene locked up her boyfriends to stop them running away,

and another where Mr Dent fell asleep when he was too drunk to find his own front door. In between the cars, the grass grew a metre high, burying all the rubbish that never quite made it to the dustbin.

As Nerlin and Merlinmary walked through the hole in the wall that had once been a gate, Rambo lifted his head over his windscreen and growled. He had a thick spiked collar around his neck and a heavy chain padlocked to the steering wheel. His eyes flashed like burning coals but it was hard to be sure he was looking at you because he was seriously cross-eyed. His sight was so wonky that he'd bitten his own leg quite a few times when he thought he was attacking the postman.

'What do you lot want?' said Mr Dent as Nerlin and

Merlinmary stood on his front step. 'Get lost, freaks.'

'There's no need to be like that,' said Nerlin. 'We'd just like to have a talk.'

'I said get lost, you weirdoes, or I'll set Rambo on you.'

'I wouldn't do that if I were you,' Nerlin warned him.

'Oh yeah, oh yeah,' said Mr Dent. 'Why not?'

'I just wouldn't,' said Nerlin.

Mr Dent unclipped Rambo's lead. The crazy dog was so desperate to get at Nerlin that he knocked Mr Dent flying, covering him in drool and dog breath, but before he could reach Nerlin, Merlinmary clicked her fingers and the giant rottweiler turned into a tiny poodle. As Mr Dent struggled to get up, Rambo the poodle shot up the inside of his trouser leg and bit him on a part of his body that should never see daylight.

'You freaks ...' Mr Dent began, but the pain was so excruciating he couldn't finish his sentence. Rambo took another bite, shot down his other trouser and raced inside the house. Mr Dent, his eyes streaming

with tears of pain, staggered to his feet and walked straight into the back bumper of Rambo's car. His pain then became serious agony as he fell over again, this time cutting his hand on a broken bottle.

'You, you, you,' he spluttered and crawled indoors, where Rambo was waiting to pay him back some more for all the kicks and swearing Mr Dent had given him over the years. As Rambo raced through every room in the Dents' house getting his revenge, it became clear why the first half of the word 'poodle' is 'poo'.

Small dogs can run a lot faster than big clumsy dogs or people. So the big clumsy Dents never managed to catch Rambo, no matter how hard they tried. They set traps baited with food, but Rambo was about three times more intelligent than they were – actually, so was the average pigeon – so they were useless.

'Nice one, sweetheart,' Nerlin said to his daughter as they left. 'First round to us, I think.'

Here
Lies
CHAPTER
6

The next day, when the Dent children were at school and Mrs Dent was in her usual place in front of the TV watching *Dr Clint's Trailer Trash Special* and Mr Dent was still asleep in bed, Rambo the poodle went to sleep in Dickie's bed. Rambo fell asleep and dreamt of the days when he'd been a puppy with all his brothers and sisters. Life had been good then, those first three months. Then he had gone to live with the Dents and it had all been downhill after that. After all those years of being chained up in a wrecked car, it was so warm and cosy in Dickie's bed – much too comfortable to get out of bed and go outside when he needed to go to the toilet.

So it doesn't take much imagination to guess

what Dickie Dent stuck his bare feet in when he got into bed that night. He didn't realise what it was straightaway. He wriggled his feet around so it went between his toes, and then the smell drifted out of the covers and hit him. At first he thought it was his mother's cooking – it wouldn't have been the first time his sister had played that trick on him – but then he realised.

'Mummmm,' he cried, but Mrs Dent had just switched channels to watch *Big Brother Special Shock Edition*, where some brain cells had been discovered in one of the contestants, and the viewers had to guess who they belonged to.

'It's them Floods' fault,' Dickie muttered. 'If they hadn't done that to Rambo …'

Dickie had always been scared out of his wits by Rambo when the dog had been a rottweiler. When he had been a baby, his dad had held him up inches away from the ferocious dog's drooling fangs, but Rambo had still been their dog and turning him into a girlie-pink poodle and making him wet Dickie's bed made him want revenge. He decided he would

wait until the Floods went out, and then go into their house and get his own back.

But as well as being a mean and nasty little boy, Dickie Dent was also very, very stupid. He was too stupid to realise that the last place on Earth you should break into was a house that belonged to a family of witches and wizards. So he waited until he saw the family leave the house for their evening walk in the local graveyard, then he kicked a hole in the fence and crawled through it and squeezed under the hedge into the Floods' back yard. The back door was unlocked so he slipped inside.

Part of Dickie's being very, very stupid was the fact that he couldn't count. When he had seen the Floods go out he hadn't made sure all nine of them were there. What made him very, very, *very* stupid was that the Flood who wasn't there was the one he actually went to school with.

The house felt creepy. The air was cold and damp, even though outside it was a warm summer's day. There weren't any chip wrappers or half-eaten burgers with mould on them like in his own kitchen.

The whole place smelled horrible.

It smelled clean.

Right, Dickie thought, *time for revenge*.

He walked over to the kitchen drawers, pulled the bottom one open and dropped his trousers.

But he was not alone. As he began to concentrate and grit his teeth, Betty tiptoed downstairs. Dickie

closed his eyes tight and began to strain. Betty had been up in her room doing her homework and had heard Dickie kicking the fence. Now, just as he was about to poo in the kitchen drawer, she made his feet give way beneath him. As Dickie fell, he grabbed hold of the nearest thing – his trousers – and pulled them up. At the last moment he realised what had happened, but he had gone too far to stop and sat down with a terrible squelch.

'Hello, Dickie,' said Betty. 'Looks like the icky bubba has pooed his pants.'

The lid flew off a jar of frogs' eyes in fish oil on the draining board and it tipped itself over Dickie's head.

'You are a clumsy little boy, aren't you?' laughed Betty as the breakfast creatures that had been hiding under the stove slithered up the boy's legs.

'I'm, I'm, I'm not scared of you,' he cried.

'Well, you should be.'

'You're just a stupid witch,' Dickie snivelled.

'Witch, yes,' said Betty. 'Stupid, no.'

The frogs' eyes slithered down his face onto his

T-shirt and looked up at him. Dickie tried to get up, but the floor was wet with fish oil and he kept slipping.

'You wait till I tell my dad,' he cried.

'Surely you don't imagine you're ever going to see your dad again, do you?' laughed Betty.

She was really enjoying herself now. A tiny bit of her brain felt a tiny little bit guilty, but she was a witch and Dickie was vile, so most of her brain said to itself: *Is this great or what?*

'Remember when your hair caught fire in class?' she said.

'That was just an accident,' said Dickie, but he knew it hadn't been. He knew Betty had made it happen.

'I don't think so,' said Betty.

Dickie's hair began to smoke and he tried to crawl towards the door, but he fell flat on his face. Betty stood over him with a sweet innocent smile on her face.

'Are you scared now?' she said.

'N-n-n-n-no,' Dickie lied.

The frogs' eyes slid up onto his face again and stared into his eyes. He began to whimper.

'You should be,' said Betty.

Dickie tried to crawl towards the door. Betty clicked her fingers and the slimy stuff Dickie was lying in began to get hotter and hotter. Two of the frogs' eyes slid up his nose and then two more. He couldn't pretend any longer. He was terrified and began to cry.

'You can say sorry now,' said Betty.

'Sorry,' he whimpered.

'I can't hear you,' said Betty.

'Sorry.'

'Louder.'

'I'm sorry. I'm sorry,' Dickie cried out. Now the tears were pouring down his face and he wet himself.

'You are a nasty evil little boy, aren't you?' said Betty.

'Yes. I'm sorry,' Dickie whimpered.

'Breaking into people's houses and doing nasty things and being vile to everyone.'

'Yes.'

'And pulling people's hair and setting fire to things and scratching people's cars.'

'Yes.'

'You're a horrible worthless piece of pig poo, aren't you?' said Betty.

'Yes … sorry,' cried Dickie.

'And you're a nasty fat little liar too, aren't you?'

'Yes.'

'And that's the main problem, really,' said Betty, 'You keep saying sorry, but you're probably lying.'

'No, I'm not, really,' pleaded Dickie.

'Really?'

'Really.'

The fish oil stopped getting hot and Dickie grabbed hold of a chair and pulled himself up.

'Can I go now?' he said.

'Promise you won't be evil any more?' said Betty.

'Yes,' said Dickie with his fingers crossed behind his back.

But he was still just as stupid as before and when he turned towards the door, he still had them crossed, so Betty could see them. It didn't matter, because there was no way Betty was letting him go.

'Stop,' she snapped and Dickie's feet stuck to the floor. 'I've changed my mind.'

'What?'

'Be afridge,' said Betty. 'Be very afridge.'

Dickie laughed that nasty little snigger that mean, evil little boys all over the world do so well.

'Don't you mean "be *afraid*", stupid?' he sneered.

'I know what I mean,' said Betty. She *had* actually meant to say, 'Be afraid,' but as often happens when people get excited, she got her words a bit muddled up. Though there was no way she was going to let Dickie know *that*.

Very slowly Dickie felt himself getting squarer. It didn't hurt at all. Betty was a witch, but she could also be

quite kind and gentle. It was something she hoped to grow out of as she got older.

Dickie stood up but he couldn't run away because his legs had sort of vanished. He still had feet – in fact he now had four of them and they were self-levelling hydraulic feet. As he looked down for what would be the last time, he thought that he actually looked nicer made of stainless steel than he had made of skin and fat. He had a gorgeous ice-cube maker in his left-hand door and a plasma TV in the right.

So, of course, Dickie died – which he definitely deserved to do, to save the world from himself – but he died happy and very shiny. His last thought was: *Wow, I am, like, the handsomest, most expensive fridge in the shop. If only Mum could see me now.*

The last thing he said was:

'Mmmmmmmmmmmmmmmmmmmmmmmmmmm mmmmmmmmmmmmmmmmmmmmmmmmm.' Which he hummed in a very soft, expensive sort of way several times a day.

'All that magic has made me really hungry,' Betty said to herself. 'I wonder what sort of stuff you get inside a fridge you've just turned someone into.'

She'd decided that Dickie would probably be empty and have to charge up overnight to get cold, until she remembered that Dickie was a magic fridge. And when Betty peered inside, he was lovely and cold and full of her favourite food. In the freezer, there were seventeen kinds of ice-cream. In the fridge, there was a huge plate of cold roast lamb with a two-litre jug of mint sauce. There were barbecued chicken wings, a sticky date pudding and a very large box of chocolates with no hard toffees at all.

Betty took out a tub of delicious strawberry ice-cream.

'Excellent,' she said, as Vlad licked the last of the fish oil off the floor.

Here
Lies
CHAPTER
7

No one in Dickie's family noticed he was missing at first. Mr and Mrs Dent didn't like their children very much, and the less they saw of them the more they liked it. Once, Tracylene had been in prison for a month for shoplifting, and her parents hadn't even noticed she'd gone.

When Mrs Dent stuck Dickie's burger, chips and beans down on the table for his tea and realised she'd just put it on top of another plate of burger, chips and beans, she wondered why her son hadn't eaten his tea the night before. She shouted upstairs for him but by the time she realised he hadn't answered, her favourite programme was on the TV, so she didn't bother. The opening music was playing and it drew

her like a magnet towards the screen.[14]

There were five plates of burger, chips and beans piled on top of each other before she thought that maybe Dickie was not at home.

'I wonder where he's got to?' she said as she sat down to watch TV again.

'Who?' said Mr Dent. 'Tracylene, get me another beer.' The beer fridge was in the hall, to be nearer to Mr Dent's TV chair, but even then, it was too much of an effort for him to fetch his own drinks.

'Get it yourself,' Tracylene shouted from her bedroom. She loved her dad in the same way people love walking in dog poo. 'I'm off out, Mum.'

'Don't do anything I wouldn't do,' Mrs Dent told her.

'You wish.'

---

[14] *Mrs Dent's favourite TV programme was* Mega-Extreme Celebrity Really Dumb Fat Ugly Stupid Idiot Loser Makeover, *where people who were dumber, fatter and even more stupid than Mrs Dent were chopped up by very, very rich doctors and turned into really thin and not-quite-as-ugly-as-before stupid idiots who couldn't believe they were still losers. It made Mrs Dent feel a lot better about herself.*

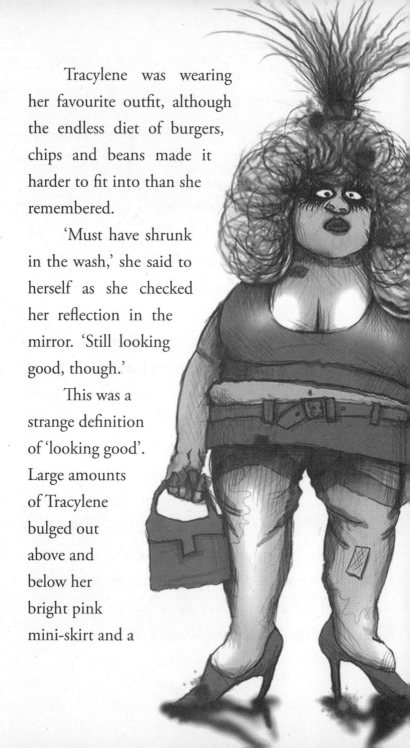

Tracylene was wearing her favourite outfit, although the endless diet of burgers, chips and beans made it harder to fit into than she remembered.

'Must have shrunk in the wash,' she said to herself as she checked her reflection in the mirror. 'Still looking good, though.'

This was a strange definition of 'looking good'. Large amounts of Tracylene bulged out above and below her bright pink mini-skirt and a large amount of her chest simply refused to stay where it was meant to. The fact that her spindly high-heeled shoes didn't collapse under her weight was proof that Chinese engineers were very clever people.

'Rubbish underwear,' she muttered, topping up her layers of eye-shadow and lipstick.

'Rubbish knickers! Rubbish knickers!' squawked Adolf the budgie, the Dent's other pet. Adolf lived in Tracylene's bedroom and she had taught him to talk. Whenever Tracylene posed in front of her mirror, which she did dozens of times a day, Adolf would whistle at her and say, 'More lipstick, baby!' and 'Nice legs!' When he was alone, though, Adolf used to look in his mirror and say to his reflection, 'It's a rotten job, but someone's got to do it.'

Tracylene tottered out of the front door and went off to meet her friends Shareelene and Torylene and a group of spotty boys who worshipped them.

After a few more days had gone by and the pile of cold burger, chips and beans had grown to eight plates high, Mrs Dent had an idea. Tomorrow she

would put the ninth plate next to the old pile instead of on top of it, just in case the pile fell over. That was the most complicated thought she'd had that month.

'He hasn't been at school all week,' she said the next night when Mr Dent got back from explaining to the dole office how his bad back had actually got a lot worse. 'Do you think we should call the police?'

'Who? Why?' asked Mr Dent. 'Tracylene, get me another beer.'

'Get it yourself,' said Tracylene, who loved her dad in the same way people love being sick. 'I'm off out, Mum.'

'Don't do anything I wouldn't do,' said Mrs Dent.

'You wish.'

Tracylene tried to imagine something her mum wouldn't do, but she couldn't.

Mrs Dent rang the police.

At first the police didn't want
to go to the Dents' house.

'That family's been nothing
but trouble since they moved
here,' Sergeant LeDouche said
after he'd got off the phone. 'The
mum's been done for dangerous
driving. The dad's been done
for drunk and disorderly. The
daughter's been done for shoplifting and the boy's always in trouble.
They're bad news.'

'Maybe if we keep quiet,'
his assistant suggested, 'they'll all
vanish one by one.'

'We can only hope so,' said
the sergeant.

But Mrs Dent kept phoning
every few days for the next month
until the police could ignore her
no longer. By the time they went
around to number 11 Acacia

67

Avenue, the kitchen table had forty-three plates of cold burger, chips and beans piled up on it. Mrs Dent had got it into her head that if she stopped putting Dickie's dinner out every day, she might never see him again.

'Okay, Mrs Dent, when did your little boy disappear?' LeDouche asked her.

'Um, one, two, three, four …' Mrs Dent tried to count the plates of cold food but got stuck when she reached seven. The sergeant could count to fifteen, which he did three times and then took two away.

'I haven't put today's dinner out yet,' said Mrs Dent. 'So that's another day.'

'Reumm, yurghhmm oh,' said the sergeant with a mouthful of cold burger.

They took away the cold dinners for forensic examination, as well as all the beers in the fridge – just in case there were fingerprints on them.

'Don't you want to see Dickie's room?' said Mrs Dent.

'Disgusting, untidy, smelly, red sports car posters, dirty clothes, wet towels, unmade bed, naughty

magazines, broken toys, is it?' said LeDouche.

'Yes, don't you want to check it for DNA?'

'Mrs Dent, we don't really do that. You've been watching too much TV.'

'Don't be stupid,' said Mrs Dent. 'How can anyone watch *too* much telly?'

'Whatever,' said the sergeant and left.

He thought about getting a missing persons poster made for Dickie, but he was such an ugly boy he decided not to because it would frighten people.

Here
Lies
CHAPTER
8

In the meantime, the Floods were enjoying their new fridge. Betty thought she might've got into trouble for what she'd done, but everyone was delighted.

'It's much better than our old fridge,' said Nerlin. 'Top of the range, excellent.'

'One less Dent in the world too,' said Valla. 'Nice one, little sister. High five.'

'No, no, Valla – remember what happened last time?' Mordonna warned him.

'What?' said Valla.

'Your hand fell off, and it took me ages to sew it back on again.'

'Isn't that supposed to happen when you do a high five?' Valla asked.

'No, not usually.'

Even Vlad the cat loved the new fridge. As he walked past it, he could see his reflection in the doors and pretend it was another cat stalking him. Also, there was a special chilled fish tank inside full of Siamese fighting fish, his favourite meal, kept at exactly the right temperature to make them really angry and fight each other as they slid down his throat.

It really was a magic fridge, with something just right for every single one of the Floods.

'I can't believe how good this chocolate intestine roll tastes,' said Merlinmary.

'And these ballerina's toes are out of this world,' Winchflat added.

'I never knew simple serial killer's blood could taste so good,' said Valla.

'Well done, sweetheart,' Nerlin said to Betty. 'We're all very proud of you.'

'It's the best sort of recycling,' said Winchflat. 'Take something broken and useless and turn it into something really useful. And I'm so glad you gave

him that special finish so we never have to polish him. Stainless steel can be really hard to keep looking nice.'

Dickie said nothing. He was a fridge, and fridges, even the most advanced ones, don't speak.[15] He just hummed softly in his expensive I'm-so-happy sort of way.

And because Dickie was a magic fridge, no matter how much of the wonderful food everyone ate, there was always more.

---

[15] *Although, I believe you'll soon be able to buy one that tells you when you need more milk or to throw out that piece of chicken that's past its use-by date, and complains when you put things it doesn't like inside it, like dead dogs and Vegemite.*

Here
Lies
CHAPTER
9

The next one to vanish was Tracylene. She was out in the back yard one night, waiting in the bushes for her second-best backup replacement boyfriend. She was wearing her new purple mini-skirt with the split up the side and an incredibly bright red lipstick she had bought off the internet that was guaranteed to drive boys wild.[16] On her feet, she wore a pair of shoes with such high heels that she had to stand on a box to put them on.

The boy, who had said his name was Jean-Claude but was actually called Graham, was lost in

---

[16] *From www.tartytat.com, which sells over-priced stuff that makes you look really cheap. Tracylene's lipstick is called Flashy Face.*

some bushes in a house over the road. Tracylene was getting so bored waiting that she'd actually started eating her nail varnish.[17] As she nibbled at her nails, not realising they were false and highly toxic, she noticed the hole that Dickie had made in the fence through to number 13.

Maybe Jean-Claude's through there, she thought and squeezed herself through into the Floods' garden. It was quiet, very, very quiet, and dark. The moon was hiding behind the trees and the only light was from the eerie strange mushrooms growing on a mound of grass by the washing line.

There were fifteen mush-rooms and they glowed like the lumi-nous letters on an old clock.

---

[17] *Another fabulous product from tartytat.com called Polyurethane Passion.*

Tracylene tottered over to the mushrooms and looked down at them. There was a sucking, popping sound as the mushroom between her feet vanished into the ground. Tracylene turned to leave but it was too late. The mound of grass was Queen Scratchrot's grave and she was having her dinner. The grave split open and a skeleton arm shot out and grabbed Tracylene around the ankle. She fell flat on her face, and before she could make a sound, a second skeleton arm stuffed one of the glowing mushrooms into her mouth and began to drag her into the grave.

While this was going on, Nerlin and Mordonna were sitting side by side on their back verandah, drinking blood-red Merlinot wine and waiting for the moon to appear. The children were all indoors watching *The World's Greatest Funerals IV* on DVD while their parents relaxed in the cool of the evening.

'Oh, look,' said Nerlin. 'Your mother's caught something.'

'That's nice,' said Mordonna. 'I wonder what it is. Looks too big to be a cat.'

'I think it's a teenage girl.'

'Oh, Mummy will be pleased,' said Mordonna. 'That's one of her favourite meals. I think it's that awful tarty girl from next door.'

'Excellent,' said Nerlin. 'Two down, two to go.'

'I hope she doesn't disagree with her, though. I imagine that family would be a bit indigestible.'

The mushroom spread its glow through Tracylene's entire body until she was shining like a big pink electric dolphin. She tried to speak, to say that she would never be a bad girl ever again if

whatever it was that had hold of her would just let her go. She tried to say she would never steal any more undies from Target or go out with bad boys or steal her mother's gin. She wanted to say that she'd always get her dad a beer when he wanted one and help her mum with whatever it was that mothers do in the kitchen room ... But no sound came out. The juice from the mushroom reached right down to the tips of her toes and began to tenderise her. Queen Scratchrot had been dead a very long time and her teeth were not as good as they used to be, so she couldn't eat anything she had to chew.

Tracylene grew softer and softer until she was like a great big human-flavoured jelly baby. She gave one final wobbly pink quiver before the ground opened up and Queen Scratchrot swallowed her. Then there was silence, followed by a very loud belch.

'That'll keep her happy for a while,' said Mordonna.

'Good thing too,' said Nerlin. 'It's getting harder and harder to catch cats for her. Even with Vlad luring them into the garden for us.'

'We can always get her another postman. She hasn't had one for ages.'

The moon rose high over the Floods' back garden. Nigel and Shirley, Valla's two pet vampire bats, went out to visit all the dogs sleeping outside in the neighbouring back yards.[18] Nerlin and Mordonna rocked gently back and forth on their verandah swing while Queen Scratchrot digested Tracylene with a chorus of burps and farts. Eventually the smell got too much.

'I'm going indoors,' said Nerlin with his hand over his nose. 'I don't know what that Dent girl has been eating but it seems to have upset your mother.'

'Do you think I should water her grave with some indigestion medicine?' Mordonna asked.

'Good idea, but whatever you do don't strike a match.'

---

[18] *Which just proves that you should always let your dog sleep inside at night. You never know when a hungry vampire bat might be around.*

Here
Lies
CHAPTER
10

Mrs Dent didn't put a plate of burger, chips and beans out for Tracylene each day like she had for Dickie. She didn't like her daughter and was quite glad she was gone.

'Great useless lump,' she said. 'She'll be back.'

'Who?' asked Mr Dent. 'Tracylene, get me another beer.'

'She's not here,' said Mrs Dent.

'Well, *you* get me one.'

'If there was any beer, I'd be able to say "Get it yourself", but the police took it all,' said Mrs Dent.

'What, you mean they *stole* it?' said Mr Dent.

'Yeah.'

'Well, I'm going to report them to the police.

They're not going to get away with it.'

Mrs Dent wasn't listening. *Pro–Celebrity See How Many Burgers You Can Eat in Five Minutes While Sitting in a Bath of Beans Championships* had just started and it was the finals. When Mr Dent rang the police station they said he could come and collect his beer, except it had mysteriously evaporated in the bottles and someone had stolen all the bottle tops.

An ad for a range of super-healthy frozen pre-cooked one-hundred-per-cent-taste-free dinners came on and Mrs Dent grabbed the phone off her husband.

'Now my daughter's gone missing too,' she told Sergeant LeDouche.

There was a silence. The sergeant was one of Tracylene's many boyfriends and he couldn't decide if he was glad she'd disappeared or if he missed her. Their relationship had always been a bit strange and difficult. For example, one night they'd been to the movies together and the next day he'd had to arrest her for shoplifting. LeDouche decided that life would be a lot less complicated if he didn't look for Tracylene too efficiently.

'Now, now, Mrs Dent,' he said. 'Don't upset yourself. I'm sure she'll turn up.'

'I'm not upset,' said Mrs Dent.

'I'll be around shortly,' he told her.

'Oh, you needn't bother,' said Mrs Dent. 'I don't particularly want you to find her.'

'Why did you phone us then?' asked the sergeant, getting suspicious.

'Well, I don't want you to think I done her in. You know, when you find her horribly mangled body somewhere.'

'Why do you think she's been horribly mangled?' said the sergeant, getting even more suspicious.

'Well, er … I don't. But when a teenager goes missing on telly they usually get horribly mangled,' said Mrs Dent, sounding more and more guilty. 'She's probably just done a runner, gone off with one of her boyfriends.'

'I think you've been watching too much TV,' LeDouche suggested.

'Don't be stupid,' said Mrs Dent. 'How can anyone watch *too much* telly?'

The sergeant arrived two minutes later and went over Tracylene's bedroom with a fine-tooth comb. He didn't find any fine teeth, but he did retrieve what he had come for: Tracylene's diary. He read the first few pages, learnt two new rude words and read some stuff that made him feel very strange. He was going to tear out the pages that contained any stuff written about him, but instead, he took the diary away to read in bed later with his cocoa.

'When did you last see your daughter?' he asked Mr and Mrs Dent.

'Dunno,' said Mr Dent. 'Get me a beer, will you?'

83

'I'll have one too,' said the sergeant.

'Get them yourself, my programme's gonna start,' said Mrs Dent.

The sergeant went back to the station and wrote his report in the special missing persons book. Not the ordinary missing persons book, but the special one with the code word on the front: CLASS (which stands for 'Complete Losers And Serial Scumbags', a special police code that meant anyone trying to find any of the people in the book would be arrested). Tracylene Dent's details were written on the page after Dickie's.

It didn't take Mr and Mrs Dent very long to forget their two children, because that was the sort of people they were. They still shouted and fought a lot and filled their garden up with more old cars and rubbish and threw empty bottles over the fence into the Floods' back garden. Even with half the family gone, the Dents were still the neighbours from hell.

'Two down, two to go,' said Valla, after Nerlin had told everyone about Tracylene.

'Which one first?' asked Mordonna. 'Him or her?'

'Well, he makes the most noise,' said Merlinmary.

'I don't know about that,' said Winchflat. 'She has the TV blaring out all day and night.'

'True,' agreed Nerlin.

'Well, we've got three choices,' said Mordonna. 'Him first, her first or both together.'

Events decided who was to be next a few weeks later. Mr and Mrs Dent had just had their usual Saturday night fight, the one where Mrs Dent ended

up locked out of the house in the back yard in her underwear in the rain while Mr Dent stayed inside with the TV up so loud he couldn't hear her. This was the only way Mr Dent ever got to watch stuff on TV that *he* wanted. He did have a TV in his shed at the bottom of the garden, but it was fifty metres from the house and the walk tired him out so much he fell asleep as soon as he got there.

Mrs Dent had done her usual screaming, throwing a brick through the window, screaming some more, beating on the back door and wailing, and now she was doing her falling down drunk in the grass and crying that no one loved her. Quite who she was trying to tell this to was a mystery. Everyone already knew that no one loved her – not

even Rambo the poodle, who, at that very moment, was attempting to kill her left slipper.

Mrs Dent tried to stand up again, landed face down in a puddle and fell asleep under a bush, with her head poking through the hole in the fence that Dickie and Tracylene had vanished through. Midnight came and went, while Mrs Dent snored like a pig with a bad sinus problem.

Apart from Betty, who slept through the night like ordinary people, the rest of the Floods barely slept. Night-time was when they did the secret special things that witches and wizards do all over the world. Spells, curses, transforming themselves into huge black bats, sucking blood, watching the shopping channels at 3 am and travelling about on broomsticks are just a few of the things that magic people prefer to do under cover of darkness.

Mrs Dent's snoring interrupted the magic flow. Mordonna's broomstick turned into a dustpan and brush. Valla spilt a glass of his finest blood all over his book of spells, with disastrous results, and Nerlin started phoning up the shopping channel to buy a hand-carved crystal mobile phone stand with 24-carat gold filigree inlay.

'Is someone trying to saw a tree down out there?' said Mordonna, relieved she had only been a metre in the air when her broomstick had changed.

'No, it's Mrs Dent snoring,' said one of the children.

'Well, it's enough to wake the dead,' said

Mordonna. 'And in our back garden that is not a good thing.'

'Oh, God no,' said Nerlin. 'It would be bad enough if your mother woke up, lovely and wonderful though she is, but if it woke Uncle Cloister, all hell would break loose.'

'Not to mention Great-Grandmother Lucreature,' said Mordonna. 'Winchflat, go out and shut the woman up, there's a good boy.'

'Temporarily or permanently?' asked Winchflat. 'With pain or without?'

'Surprise us,' said Nerlin.

Winchflat went out into the garden and found Mrs Dent's head sticking through the fence. She was now lying on her back in a patch of stinging nettles with her mouth wide open. As usual her lipstick was smeared all over the place, looking as if it was trying to escape. Winchflat picked up two handfuls of earth and dropped them into Mrs Dent's mouth.

Mrs Dent choked, spluttered and opened her eyes. The skinny, sickly figure of Winchflat towering overhead scared the living daylights out of her, and

she screamed as loud as someone with a mouthful of earth can scream. Which is not at all. She rolled onto her front, spat out the earth and escaped back into her own garden. The last thing she saw as she wriggled away was something red and shiny. It was half hidden by Winchflat's long spindly legs, but there was no mistaking what she had seen.

It was one of Tracylene's red high-heeled shoes.

She had a brief flash of nearly being almost-but-not-quite intelligent and said nothing. She wriggled backwards through the fence, but it was too late. Winchflat realised she had seen the shoe.

'She'll have to go,' said Mordonna when Winchflat got back inside.

'How on Earth did we miss the shoes?' said Nerlin.

'I don't know. Mother must have regurgitated them,' said Mordonna.

'I thought she liked shoes.'

'Not red ones,' said Mordonna. 'They give her wind.'

Mrs Dent staggered towards her back door, spitting out the earth and crying. It wasn't knowing her daughter was probably dead that made her so hysterical. Nor was it the terrifying experience she'd just had with Winchflat. No, it was the realisation that she'd been asleep for three hours and had missed the final ever episode of *Mega-Extreme Celebrity Really Dumb Fat Ugly Stupid Idiot Loser Makeover*, where they were going to replace someone's entire brain with a silicone implant. She had been looking forward to it all week, and now, quite simply, her life was ruined.

As it was Saturday night, she did what she

always did after the big row with her husband and began wailing at the back door until Mr Dent, who was passed out under the kitchen table in his usual Saturday night pool of sick, woke up and let her back inside. Then Mr and Mrs Dent spent half an hour crying and telling each other how much they loved each other and how they would never be horrible to each other ever again until next Saturday.

When she woke up at three o'clock the next afternoon, Mrs Dent remembered the red shoes and reached for the phone.

Sergeant LeDouche was sleeping when the phone rang. Since Dickie and Tracylene had disappeared, Saturday nights had been a lot more relaxed. No one had thrown any bricks through the police station window. And without Tracylene telling him how much she loved him as she threw up into his police helmet every Friday night, he managed to get a lot more sleep during his weekend shifts. Now

that bloody woman was on the phone again.

'Sergeant,' Mrs Dent cried down the phone, 'them weirdoes next door killed my daughter, er, er ...'

'Tracylene,' said the sergeant.

'Yeah, her,' said Mrs Dent. 'I saw her shoe in their back garden.'

'Okay, I'll look into it.'

Here
Lies
CHAPTER
12

Sergeant LeDouche had never been to the Floods' house, nor had he ever wanted to. The place gave him the creeps, but after Mrs Dent's call about the shoes, he had no choice. If there was actual evidence of foul play, then Dickie and Tracylene's disappearances could no longer be ignored and would have to be looked into. He would have to rub out their entries in the CLASS book and rewrite them in the proper missing persons book, the one that meant he had to do something, like investigating or covering everything up – whichever was the easiest.

He parked his police car down the street outside number 21 and walked back to the Floods' gate. It opened a split second before he touched it and closed

as soon as he was through. He turned to open it again but it growled at him.

'Come in, Forty-Two,' he said into his walkie-talkie. 'Forty-Two' was his nickname for his sidekick, who was waiting in the car. (His real name was Forty-One – Peter Lawrence Henry Forty-One, to be precise.)

'Hello, Sarge,' said Forty-Two.

'The front gate just growled at me, Forty-Two,' said the sergeant.

'Of course it did, Sarge.'

The sergeant could have sworn he heard the gate laughing, but he decided not to tell Forty-Two about that. He walked up the path to the front door and, a split second before his finger reached it, the bell rang. The door opened and something small, dark and very hairy stood there wagging its back end. It was Satanella.

'What do you want?' asked Satanella.

'Err, um,' said the sergeant, looking down the hall to see who was talking to him.

'Down here,' said Satanella. 'I may look like a dog, but that doesn't mean I am one. What do you want?'

'Right, yes, okay … Is your, er, master or mistress in?' LeDouche asked her, not believing he was actually talking to a dog. He just hoped no one could see him.

'Wait there,' said Satanella and scampered off down the hall.

'Forty-Two, you still there?'

'Yes, Sarge.'

'A dog just spoke to me. It actually said proper words and –'

'Well, well, that's nice,' said Forty-Two into the car radio while he reached for his mobile phone. He wondered how long it would take for an ambulance and a doctor with a powerful sedative and a straightjacket to arrive.

'Good afternoon,' said Mordonna, appearing from nowhere. 'What can we do for you?'

Sergeant LeDouche was captivated. Mordonna had deliberately left her sunglasses off and it's a well-known fact that anyone who looks into her eyes falls hopelessly head over heels in love with her. Nerlin did it several times a day.

'I um, er, um,' the sergeant stammered, and followed Mordonna into the kitchen like a devoted puppy.

'Sit down and tell me what the problem is,' said Mordonna.

'Well, my wife doesn't understand me, my Vicki's doing badly at school and I've started to go bald,' the sergeant began.[19]

'No, no. I mean, why are you here?'

'Oh, that is so true. *Why* am I here?' said the sergeant. 'Why is any of us here? What does it all *mean*?'

'No, why have you come to my house?' said Mordonna.

'Shoes,' the sergeant replied. 'Red shoes.'

'These shoes?' said Mordonna, holding up the high heels.

'Tracylene's shoes.'

---

[19] *Actually, the sergeant's wife understood him only too well. Their daughter Vicki had been in the same class at school as Tracylene, so Mrs LeDouche knew all about what he'd been up to.*

'Yes, that nasty little girl.' Mordonna's eyes narrowed as she spoke. She put her sunglasses on and released the policeman from her enchanting powers.

'My mother enjoyed her very much,' she added.

'Your mother?' said LeDouche.

'Yes, my mother. She's buried in the back garden. Do you want to meet her?'

'Meet her? Buried ... she's *dead*?'

'Of course she's dead,' said Mordonna. 'You don't bury people when they're alive, do you?'[20]

'Yeah but, no but – excuse me a minute. I have to talk to my partner.' Switching on his walkie-talkie, the sergeant hurried out into the hall.

'Forty-Two, are you there?'

'Er, yes,' Forty-Two replied cautiously. The ambulance was still ten minutes away so he had to play for time.

---

[20] *Mordonna's uncle, Count Septic Von Pus, had actually been buried alive as a birthday present one year and had liked it so much he had stayed buried for the next fifty years until he died. Then he was dug up and cremated.*

'I need a team of officers with shovels,' LeDouche told him.

'Of course you do,' said Forty-Two slowly.

'I think the girl's buried in the back garden and I believe they might have buried an old lady there too, while she was still alive,' said the sergeant.

'Okay. Excellent. Well done, Sarge,' said Forty-Two. 'There aren't any more talking animals or gates, are there?'

'No, no. Just phone for back-up, like I told you,' LeDouche ordered.

'No worries, Sarge. I've done that already. They should be here in a few minutes. You just play for time.'

'Okay, that's sorted out then,' said the sergeant, walking back into the Floods' kitchen. 'Any chance of a cup of tea?'

'Tea? Tea? I don't think we've got any tea,' Mordonna replied. 'Got a nice drop of chilled bat's blood.'

'No, that's fine. I'll just have a glass of water.'

'Okay. Have a nice glass of chilled water from

100

our lovely new fridge,' said Mordonna. 'Would you like a frog's eye in it?'

'No, it's all right. I'm not actually that thirsty,' said the sergeant. 'Maybe we could have a look in the back garden.'

'Yes, of course. I was telling Mother about you while you were on the phone just then. Follow me.'

They walked outside and there, as Mordonna had said, was a grave, right in the middle of the lawn next to the clothesline.

'This is the policeman I was telling you about, Mother,' Mordonna shouted down at the grave. There was silence for a moment. 'Oh, all right, Mother.'

Turning back to LeDouche, she added, 'Sorry I had to shout. Mother's a bit deaf. She wants to shake your hand.'

'Of course she does,' said the sergeant and walked over to the grave side.

The ground opened and a skinny skeleton arm appeared.

'Mother says just shake her hand. She only lets wizards kiss it.'

The sergeant fainted.

When Forty-Two, three large ambulance men and a doctor arrived five minutes later, Sergeant LeDouche was lying on the couch in the Floods' lounge room. He was mumbling to himself and dribbling into his walkie-talkie.

'I'm terribly sorry about all this, madam,' said the doctor. 'It's the strain of the job.'

'I understand,' said Mordonna from behind her dark glasses.

Satanella made pretend happy little yappy dog noises as one of the ambulance men tickled her

tummy. The doctor gave the sergeant a powerful sedative and then they took him away to the mad house in a straightjacket. His wife and children decided they'd be happier with Forty-Two, who had just been promoted and didn't look like the sort of man who would have other girlfriends.

Sergeant LeDouche spent a very long time resting and being given large doses of strange medicine and electric shock treatment at the Sunshine Home for the Really Stressed before getting a pension and going off to live all alone by the sea in a small damp flat with no waterfront views. Now and then over the following years, there were nights when he would wake up screaming, because he knew what he had heard and seen had not been in his imagination. And he knew without a doubt that the Floods had killed Tracylene, and probably Dickie, and that

they had cut off his brilliant career long before it had reached its peak.

Thoughts of revenge grew dark and evil in his heart. Somehow, somewhere, he would pay them back.

Here
Lies
CHAPTER
13

A couple of months after the sergeant had been taken away, Mrs Dent went into Tracylene's old bedroom and remembered that she'd once had a daughter. Mr Dent had already filled Dickie's old room with bits of old motorbike, some buckets of grease and twelve hundred and twenty-seven empty beer cans. But apart from taking Tracylene's budgie, Adolf, down to the kitchen – where he got fatter and fatter and fatter on a diet of pizza crusts and kept telling Mr Dent he needed more lipstick – neither parent had been in her room since.

I wonder what happened to Tracylene, Mrs Dent thought, and then she remembered the red shoes.

She rang the police station, but since the sergeant had been taken away they had decided on a new policy and that was to pretend the Dents did not exist. The whole family had just been in the sick sergeant's imagination.

'I'm sorry, madam,' they said to Mrs Dent. 'The case is closed.'

'But my daughter,' said Mrs Dent. 'She's missing.'

'Congratulations,' said the policeman and put the phone down.

Mrs Dent wasn't that bothered – she was more interested in finding out if there was a fattest budgie in the world category in the *Guinness World Records* TV show – but that night when most of the world was asleep, she forced herself through the hole in the fence into the Floods' back garden.

It was as quiet as the grave, which wasn't really surprising considering how many people were buried there. Incredibly, the red shoes were still there. Mrs Dent took off her slippers and put them on. She would have thought about the story of Cinderella,

except 'Cinderella' was much too big a word to fit inside her head.

Upstairs in one of the back bedrooms, Winchflat, the family's computer genius, was doing what he did most nights: following strange people around the world on the internet. As midnight fell in one chat room, he moved on to the next time zone. On the net Winchflat was a legend. He could hack into anything and had once made the whole of America bankrupt in a single night, just for the fun of it. He put all the money back the next day, but not before three hundred and four crooked accountants and bank managers had committed suicide – a bonus even he hadn't imagined. He made all the poor people a bit richer and all the rich people quite a bit poorer. Of course it was all hushed up, but all the super-hackers knew Winchflat (or Naughty Trixie, as he was known on the net) had been there.

The night Mrs Dent came into their back garden, Winchflat was standing by the window drinking a can of Super-High-Caffeine-Zap-A-Cola when he looked down and saw her stumbling about

on the lawn in the red high heels they had left there as bait. He immediately went and told the others.

'The hippo has landed.'

'Okay,' said Nerlin, 'but we still have to decide what to do with her.'

'Mummy's hungry,' said Mordonna.

'No, that's boring,' said Morbid. Silent nodded vigorously.

'We want something we can all enjoy,' said Satanella. 'Anyway, all that fat wouldn't be good to eat, even for someone as dead as Granny.'

'Something artistic,' Betty suggested. She was

the creative one in the family. 'Maybe we could turn her into a fruit tree, or a hot tub.'

'Can you imagine what the fruit would taste like?' said Valla. 'Yuck. Quite like the hot tub idea, though. I mean, she's a great big tub already.'

'No, no, I've got it,' said Nerlin. 'What did the wretched woman do that annoyed us the most?'

'Breathe?' said Winchflat.

'No, *keep her TV blaring out all day and night.* So let's turn her into a super deluxe flat-screen plasma television.'

'Can we have surround sound with all the loudspeakers around the room?'

'Absolutely,' said Nerlin.

'Can *we* do it?' asked the twins.

'No, me, me!' said Merlinmary.

'We'll draw straws,' Nerlin decided. 'Everyone get a pencil and paper, and whoever draws the longest straw can do the magic.'

(You might be wondering why Nerlin didn't just do the magic himself. Well, I'm going to let you in on a very secret secret that no one who isn't a wizard or witch

knows. It will also explain why Nerlin took Merlinmary with him when he went to talk to Mr Dent, and why it was Merlinmary who turned Rambo into a poodle. Before I do, you must promise inside your head that you will never tell this secret to anyone else.

If you look at all the stories about wizards from Merlin through to Harry Potter, you will see that not many of them get married and have children. You might think this is because most wizards are seriously ugly, but that's not the case. Most witches actually think wizards look really cool and handsome. No, the reason is this: when a wizard is born he has magical powers, but if he has a child, that child takes some of his parent's magical powers. And as the child grows so do his magical powers, but the bit his father gave him is not replaced. This means that Nerlin, who has had seven children, has lost a lot of his magic.

It doesn't matter how the children are made – in a laboratory, grown from a cutting or made like you and I were – the wizard always loses a bit of his power.

Now the only thing that Nerlin can turn people into is a potted plant. He has even lost the power to

make them become frogs or toads.

When people call him Merlin, which they do all the time, he explains that 'N' comes after 'M' and he came after Merlin so that was why he was called Nerlin. Sensible people look confused at this, and just nod. Stupid people look sarcastic and ask him why his sons aren't called Oerlin, Perlin and Qerlin, then. These people usually get turned into geraniums.

'Couldn't you try to turn them into useful herbs, like parsley and mint and deadly nightshade?' Mordonna would ask. 'I hate geraniums, with all their horrible bright happy flowers.'

The Floods are a very close, loving family so they make sure that no outsiders ever discover Nerlin's secret. They're not likely to anyway. Nerlin is very tall, wears a big black cloak and looks seriously evil. Only complete idiots ever say, 'You haven't got any magical powers' – and they're better off as potted plants anyway.

Nerlin's loss of powers do make him quite depressed, though. 'I've lost my magic,' he says to Mordonna when they're alone. 'How can you love a man with no magic?'

'You'll always be magic to me, my darling,' Mordonna reassures him. 'Have you thought of potted chrysanthemums? They're much nicer than geraniums, and they're the flower of death too.'

'I don't choose geraniums deliberately, my angel,' Nerlin explains. 'I try to make other plants but they always turn out geraniums. I hate geraniums.'

The obvious solution would have been for Mordonna to turn them into other plants herself. She could have done it easily, but she never did. It would have made Nerlin even more depressed.)

Betty drew the longest and most artistic-looking straw, so she got to do the trick. She opened the back door.

'Hello, Mrs Hippo,' she said.

Mrs Dent tripped over her heels and fell flat on her face. Queen Scratchrot's arms poked out of her grave and started waving around.

'DROP IT!' shouted Betty before her granny could get a grip. 'Are you looking for something, Mrs Hippo?'

'You killed my Tracylene, didn't you?' said

Mrs Dent, struggling to her feet. She started to limp towards the house. One of the high heels had broken off so she walked with a ridiculous limp that made the whole family burst out laughing. 'I'll get youse!'

'Yes, you will,' said Betty. 'You'll get us lots of

lovely wildlife documentaries and fancy films with subtitles.'

'And *World's Funniest Funerals*,' said Morbid.

'And *Animal Hospital*,' said Satanella.

'And great cookery programmes, too,' said Mordonna.

'And *no* reality shows at all,' said Winchflat.

Mordonna put her arm around Betty and said, 'Look, darling, I know you drew the best straw, but maybe you better let someone else do the magic. You know how your tricks sometimes don't work out quite how you plan them, and we don't want her turned into a cabin cruiser or a hot-air balloon.'

'She's one of them already, Mummy,' said Betty, and they all laughed again, which made Mrs Dent even redder in the face.

'Better make sure there's a control to turn the colour down,' Valla added and then everyone laughed so much their sides began to ache.

They waited until Mrs Dent reached the house. Big flat-screen TVs are quite heavy and they wanted their victim to be as close as possible, so they wouldn't

have to carry her too far. Mrs Dent hobbled across the verandah and lunged for the door. As she tripped and fell inside, Winchflat clicked his fingers. There was a quick flash and a split second later she turned into a television – and not a plasma one, but an LCD, which has a much better picture.

'Brilliant,' said the twins.

'And viewable from a very wide angle,' said Nerlin.

'She'd need to be,' Betty laughed.

'Stop it, stop it,' cried Mordonna. 'If I laugh any more I'll wet myself.'

'Yeewwww, Mum, too much information,' said Morbid.

'The sound from the bass speakers is making my fur stand on end,' said Satanella.

The whole family sat up for the rest of the night watching really old horror movies and the shopping channel, which is all that's on at that time of day. Winchflat said he'd work on it so they'd be able to get every single channel in every single country on Earth – which would mean they could watch really old

horror movies and shopping channels in hundreds of different languages.[21]

'Three down, one to go,' said Mordonna, cuddling up to Nerlin. 'This couch is a bit lumpy. You know, I think it's time we got a new one.'

'As you said, one to go.'

---

[21] *Which is just like satellite TV, only they wouldn't have to pay for it.*

Here
Lies
CHAPTER
14

Mr Dent didn't notice his wife had gone until the following night.

Something wasn't right. He could sense it, but he couldn't put his finger on it. It was only a subtle change and Mr Dent didn't do subtle. Then it dawned on him. It was the smell.

As always, every single square centimetre of the house smelled of burgers, chips and beans. Over the years, layer upon layer of scented grease had built up until everything, even freshly washed clothes and Adolf the budgie's feathers, smelled the same. The smell oozed out of every pore of the Dents' skin. Even if they had used a deodorant – which was about as likely as finding intelligent life on Mars or *Big*

Brother – their armpits would still have smelled of burgers, chips and beans. The only good thing about everything smelling of burgers, chips and beans was that it covered up the terrible smell of Mr Dent's disgusting socks and bad breath. This endless diet of grease with bits of gristle and other rubbish added had covered Mr Dent's back with so many angry pimples it looked like a map of Patagonia, except the mountains weren't all green. Some were purple. If gross and disgusting had been in the Olympics, Mr Dent would have won triple gold.

But that night, something was missing. The smell was slightly different. Instead of a new cloud of hot greasy mist hovering in the air, there was just the old cold smell like first thing in the morning. Except now it was the evening.

'Oi,' he shouted.

'Oi' was what Mr and Mrs Dent called each other when they weren't fighting.

'Oi, where's me dinner? Get us a beer.'

Silence.

'I said, where's me dinner?' he shouted.

More silence, interrupted by the sound of Rambo scratching at the back door. Mr Dent fell asleep again but ten minutes later the dog's barking woke him up and he did something he hadn't done for years, except when he was too drunk to know where he was. He went into the kitchen.

'Blimey, what's all this stuff?' he said, looking at the kettle and the stove and the toaster. 'Women's toys, I suppose.'

Mrs Dent wasn't there. Nor was she in the bedroom, the bathroom or the back yard. Mr Dent didn't look in the garage or his shed because women were not allowed in there. The more he didn't find Mrs Dent the more angry he became. His neck got redder and redder, and even three beers didn't help. Six more beers didn't help either. Soon his neck got as red as a traffic light and Rambo, mistaking him for a gigantic frankfurter, bit his ankle.

Mr Dent staggered back to his chair and fell asleep again while *Pro–Celebrity Wife Swap USA* started. This made him even more bad-tempered because it was his favourite programme. He would

often daydream about swapping Mrs Dent for a big red sports car and then fall asleep and have a nightmare where he'd swapped her for her mother.

It was dark when he woke up and his stomach was calling out for burger, chips and beans.

'Oi, where's me dinner? Get us a beer,' he shouted.

Silence.

But he was not alone. There was a tall figure silhouetted in the glow from the television. She clicked her fingers and the TV fell silent.

'Hello, Mr Dent,' said Mordonna. 'Mrs Dent isn't here. Why don't you come and have dinner at our house?'

Mr Dent tried to get up but he was too drunk and there was a terrible pain in his right foot. Rambo, who hadn't had any dinner either, had bitten off his big toe and was lying under the coffee table chewing it.

Mr Dent started to sweat but Mordonna took off her dark glasses and he was totally hypnotised. Her eyes glowed like fire and Mr Dent was as feeble

as a puppy – a drunk, ugly, stupid puppy, but a puppy nevertheless.

'We've got beer, lovely and cold, in our great big new fridge,' Mordonna murmured.

'Beer?' said Mr Dent.

'Yes, and you can watch soccer on our massive new flat-screen TV,' said Betty, who was standing next to her mother.

Mr Dent opened his mouth, but no words came out.

'Do you know what the time is?' Mordonna asked him.

Mr Dent could only shake his head.

'It's time for a change. It's time for you to do something useful.'

'Uhhh?' Mr Dent managed to say.

'Have you ever done any housework?' said Mordonna. Then she clicked her fingers and gave Mr Dent back the power of speech.

'Do I look like a woman?' he snorted. 'Of course I haven't.'

'Well, it's time to start,' said Betty. 'This place is a pigsty, without the intelligent pigs. And you are disgusting.'

Mr Dent had fallen off the chair. He was now crawling blindly around on the floor on his hands and knees while Rambo tried to bite off his other big toe.

'Mr Piggy is a filthy little piggy, isn't he, Betty?' said Mordonna.

'Yes, Mother. He should be a cleaner –'

Betty had intended to say, 'He should be

a cleaner piggy', but as soon as she said the word 'cleaner', there was a flash of light that cut off her words.

The pain in Mr Dent's right foot vanished. It happened so suddenly he sat up and looked at his feet. Then he fainted.

Mr Dent's feet weren't feet any more. They were wheels – small, round, shiny wheels. He woke up, became very suddenly sober and screamed.

'Shhh, you'll wake the neighbours,' said Mordonna. 'Oh, we *are* the neighbours, and we're awake already.'

Then Mr Dent felt himself shrinking and changing shape. His skin was changing too. Now it wasn't what you'd call skin, it was what you'd call stainless steel.

'Oops,' said Betty. 'Sorry, Mother. Think I got it wrong again.'

'Don't apologise, darling,' said Mordonna. 'The stainless steel matches the fridge and the TV surround. I can see a family resemblance.'

Betty and Mordonna both collapsed on the floor laughing while Mr Dent sat there terrified. His legs seemed to have vanished up into his body and he couldn't move.

'Help,' he bleated.

'What's the matter?' said Mordonna. 'We stopped your foot hurting, didn't we?'

Betty walked over to Mr Dent and patted him on the head.

'There, there,' she said. 'Just look on the bright side – and all your sides are bright now – we've cured your spots.'

With that, mother and daughter fell about laughing again.

A few seconds later the transformation was complete. What had once been a fat, lazy pig of a man was now the best vacuum cleaner in the world. Mr Dent was the ultimate vacuum cleaner. He was a cordless automatic robot vacuum cleaner that could back his bottom up to an electric socket and plug himself in whenever his batteries started going flat. While everyone was resting or out, Mr Dent went quietly and efficiently around the whole house, stairs included, sucking up dust. He even had an extra-long nozzle that got cobwebs off the ceiling and a special attachment for getting Satanella's and Merlinmary's hair off the furniture. And when his bag was full, Mr

Dent went out into the garden and emptied himself into the bin, before starting the whole thing all over again.

Now, in a normal house, getting all the dusting and cleaning done automatically would be great. But it wasn't like that in the Floods' house. The Floods had cobwebs that were old friends. Generations of spiders had lived in complete safety on the ceilings and windows, knowing that no one was ever going to come and sweep them away. They had dust collected in happy piles around the house that just moved to one side when anyone needed to go past.

If Betty hadn't made another mistake, Mr Dent would now be a big comfy sofa – though Mordonna had to admit, the thought of sitting in Mr Dent's ex-lap was a bit creepy. With magic that was meant to happen, it was always possible to change your mind, but because Betty's magic was so uncontrolled, no one knew the formula, which made changing it pretty dangerous. If they made a mistake, Mr Dent could turn into something covered in mould that smelled like a bad drain and kept exploding. On the other hand, he could change into something awful.

So once again Winchflat, the family genius, sorted things out. He took the Dent-O-Vac down to his special workshop in the cellars and made a few modifications. Basically, he made Mr Dent run backwards (which anyone who had known him as a human would have said he'd done all his life). Every morning Mr Dent trundled out into the garden and collected dust and flies. Then he spent the rest of the day spreading the dust around the house and feeding the flies to the spiders. At midnight, when

his work was done, he would trundle into the kitchen and sit next to Dickie the fridge and the two of them would hum softly together in a very loving father and son bonding way, which they had never done when they were human.

Once the final Dent had been taken care of, Rambo's evil spell was broken and he became a cuddly, fluffy, happy little poodle. He went to live with the nice neighbours at number 15 – an old couple who spoilt him rotten with poached chicken, crispy liver treats and a red velvet cushion to sleep on.

Mordonna turned the Dents' other pet, Adolf the budgie, into a small solar-powered lawnmower, to trim the grass on Queen Scratchrot's grave. That way he would always be close to Tracylene.

Here
Lies
CHAPTER
15

When you are as dreadful as the Dents were, all your relatives pretend they don't know you. Sometimes they move to another town and sometimes they even move to Patagonia. No one knew if the Dents had any relatives, but if they did, they were never found.[22] There was a rumour that, rather than have anyone know they were related to them, their cousins had gone to live in a remote shack high up in the Andes. So when the final Dent had been 're-assigned', as Mordonna described it, no one missed them. There was even talk of a big party in the street to celebrate.

---

[22] *If you had relatives like the Dents, would you admit it?*

If a family of nice people disappeared, the place would be crawling with detectives with big torches looking for clues. They would fingerprint every square centimetre of the house, even inside the toilet bowl. They would scrape DNA out of the bottom of the garbage bin trying to find out what had happened. No stone would be left unturned.

But when the Dents all vanished, the police raced into action by buying the biggest bottle of champagne they could find and celebrating for three days. They put the news in their monthly newsletter, in the 'Good News' section, and everyone kept their fingers crossed just to make sure the Dents wouldn't come back.

After a couple of months, the bank, who owned nearly all of the house, put up a 'For Sale' sign. The house would be auctioned in a week's time.

'I hope the next owners are all right,' said Betty.

'Mmmm,' said Nerlin.

'What?' said Mordonna. 'Have you got a plan?'

'Well,' said Nerlin, 'there is a way to make *sure* we like the new owners.'

'How?'

'We become the new owners,' said Nerlin.

'You mean, move next door?' asked Betty. 'But who will live here?'

'We will,' said Nerlin. 'Look, there's nine of us, not to mention the corpses and ghosts. We could do with more room.'

So that's what they did.

If you went to an auction and saw a family that looked like the Floods standing there, you'd have to be pretty brave to bid against them. And if you saw how spooky and weird the Floods' house and garden were next door, you probably wouldn't want to live there anyway. Because of this, there were very few people at the auction outside number 11 Acacia Avenue. There was the standard property developer, who wanted to pull the house down and build a

block of flats, and there were five people who had seen all the junk in the front garden and thought it was a garage sale.

Mordonna went up to the property developer and whispered in his ear. But he just walked off in silence.

'What did you say to him?' asked Nerlin.

'I asked him if he had ever thought what life would be like if he had sticky feet and could cling to glass,' said Mordonna.

The auctioneer climbed up on a box and held up his hand.

'Who will start the bidding?' he said.

'Two hundred and fif –' the property developer started to say, but before he could finish, Mordonna clicked her fingers. There was a gentle plop and the property developer decided that he'd rather spend the rest of his life eating flies and hopped off into the grass.

Then there was silence.

'Come on,' said the auctioneer. 'Who will give me three hundred thousand?'

'Twelve dollars,' Betty called out.

'Twelve dollars? *Twelve* dollars?' said the auctioneer. 'Come on, people. This house has to be sold today.'

'I'll give you four dollars for the old washing machine,' said one of the five bargain hunters.

'I've changed my mind,' said Betty. 'Ten dollars.'

More nervous silence.

The auctioneer would have cried, except people who sell houses can't cry, because the bits of their

brains that have feelings have been removed.

'Two hundred thousand, please?'

Silence, followed by everyone except the Floods walking nervously back to their cars.

'One hundred thousand … please?'

A very long silence.

'Who bid ten dollars?' the auctioneer asked.

'I did,' said Betty.

'You're too young.'

'Ten dollars and five cents,' said Betty. 'And if you check part III, subsection 18, page 735 of volume 47 of the house owning code, I think you'll find that anyone over the age of two is allowed to buy a house.'

This, of course, was completely made up, but the auctioneer didn't know that. And anyway, he realised that ten dollars and five cents was better than no dollars and the disgrace of being the first auctioneer ever in the whole town to not sell a house at auction.

'Okay, okay, any advance on ten dollars and five cents?' he said.

The auctioneer waited for fifteen minutes, shuffling his feet and trying not to cry onto his clipboard. He knew no one was going to make a better offer. He knew he was now in Auctioneer-Nightmare-Land.[23] Finally he couldn't delay it any longer. He lifted his shaking hand and said, 'Ten dollars and five cents – going once, going twice, going three times … gone.'

Betty gave him ten dollars and ten cents and said he could keep the change, and the Floods promised they would never tell anyone how much they had paid for the house.

---

[23] *Where ALL auctioneers deserve to go.*

Here
Lies
CHAPTER
16

The Floods got back the ten dollars and ten cents by selling all the rubbish in the Dents' front garden to the garage sale man for twenty-five dollars. The garage sale man came with a big truck and took away all the old cars, washing machines, fridges, bottles and other junk. He thought he'd got the bargain of the century. The Floods *had* got the bargain of the century and after the impromptu garage sale now had a tidy front garden and enough money left over for each of them to buy a lottery ticket which, because they could do magic, won them just enough money to be called 'wow' but not enough to make the newspapers interested.

The school holidays began and the whole Flood

family spent the next two weeks having a backyard and indoors blitz until the ex-Dent house was perfect. It took some very powerful magic to shift all the layers of burger grease that covered everything. It was impossible to make it vanish completely. The best they could do was gather it all up in one big ball of fat and send it across the other side of the world to a small tropical island where people still talk of the day the giant asteroid of lard from the great chip shop in the heavens landed on their beach. They see it as proof that they are the Chosen People.

'Now we've got all this extra space,' Mordonna said, 'maybe I should have another baby.'

'Err, umm, I'm just going down to my shed,' said Nerlin. He had taken over Mr Dent's shed and was discovering all the wonderful things that blokes did in their sheds, like sitting around in dirty old armchairs listening to broken radios and drinking beer while they rubbed oil into lots and lots of spanners and chisels that they would never use for anything.

The twins pulled down the fence between the

two back gardens, giving the family enough room to bury several more dead relatives who had come with them from Transylvania Waters and had been stored in old jam jars in one of the deepest cellars with only the night eels[24] for company.

'Great idea,' said Mordonna. 'Mother's been complaining that she's got no one to talk to apart from the worms, and now that they've eaten the last bits of her skin, even they don't visit her any more.'

They decided to bring in one dead relative from each side of the family – Great-Aunt Blodwen and Uncle Flatulence. When they had settled in, they'd bury a couple more.

'I've got a soft spot for Great-Aunt Blodwen,' said Nerlin. 'It's over there by the new vegie garden.'

Winchflat built another one of his brilliant machines – the iCellar, Dungeon and Moat Replicator[25] – which photocopied all the tunnels and cellars under the Floods' house, turned them

---

[24] *See the back of this book.*
[25] *Because the Floods don't live in a castle, they keep their moat in thousands of bottles in the wine cellar.*

back to front and moved them under the Dents' old house and then joined the two sets up. Merlinmary connected everything up to her lead-lined bed and even strung some black fairy lights around Nerlin's shed.

They decided to keep both kitchens because everyone agreed they would be much happier if Satanella had somewhere to eat where the others didn't have to watch, smell or hear her.

As the school holidays came to an end, Valla gave the windows their final coat of dust and black paint, Betty planted the last patch of poison ivy in the flower beds and the other children spent two frantic days doing all the wizard school homework they should have done two weeks before.

The last day of the holidays was, like it is everywhere, weird. It was still the holidays so you could do what you liked, but whatever you did never seemed that great because you knew tomorrow you'd be back at school.

The whole family sat on the back verandah drinking warm blood slurpies as the ice-cold moon

rose over the trees and cast its peaceful light over the two fresh graves.

'Listen to that,' said Mordonna.

'What? I can't hear anything,' said Nerlin.

'Exactly.'

Life, at last, was perfect.

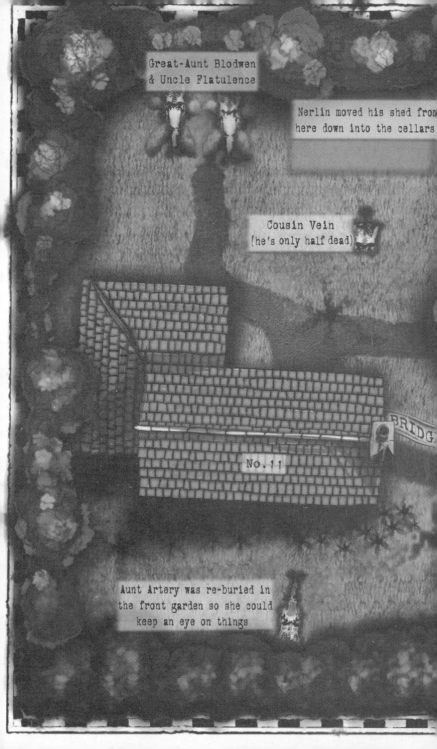

This one was here when the Floods moved in

QUEEN SCRATCHROT'S GRAVE

Great-Grandmother Lucreature

Uncle Cloister

No.13

11 & 13 ACACIA AVENUE

The
Flood
Family
Files

NERLIN

Nerlin is the great-great-grandson of Merlin, the most famous wizard who ever lived. He would have been called Merlin but at his Devilling (like a Christening for wizards) the priest had a terrible cold.

- Likes - Square tables.
- Dislikes - Round tables and people called Arthur, and drains.
- Hobbies - Stamp collecting.
- Pets - None of his own, but takes care of everyone else's.
- Favourite colour - Transparent.
- Favourite food - Banquets.

MORDONNA

In the world of witchcraft and magic, Mordonna is a legend. Magicians and wizards fall at her feet just to smell the dirt between her toes. Every single month since its very first issue, she has been Magic Monthly's centrefold pin-up. Yet for all her staggering beauty and mystery, she is an unspoilt down-to-earth housewife who likes nothing more than a quiet evening at home with her family sucking the insides out of lizards and watching Susan the Teenage Human on TV.

- Likes - Her family.
- Dislikes - Cats and cardigans.
- Hobbies - Knitting cardigans ~~for~~ from cats.
- Pets - Nerlin and a senile vulture called Leach.
- Favourite colour - Red.
- Favourite food - Diet blood.

(Leach flew in through the
window the day Mordonna
was born and has been her
devoted slave ever since.
Now he is so old, someone
else has to pre-chew his
carrion for him. You don't
want to know who that is,
but their name rhymes with
Jack Donalds.)

VALLA - 22

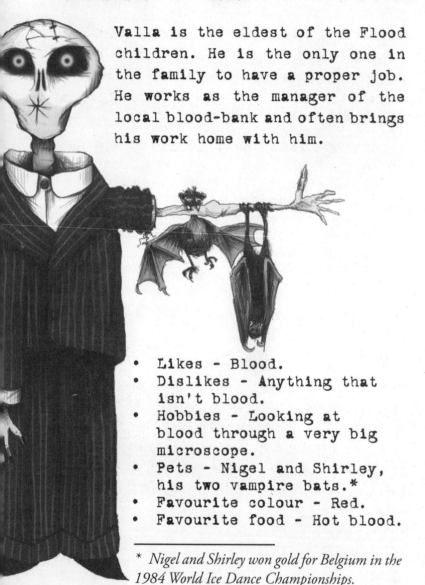

Valla is the eldest of the Flood children. He is the only one in the family to have a proper job. He works as the manager of the local blood-bank and often brings his work home with him.

- Likes - Blood.
- Dislikes - Anything that isn't blood.
- Hobbies - Looking at blood through a very big microscope.
- Pets - Nigel and Shirley, his two vampire bats.*
- Favourite colour - Red.
- Favourite food - Hot blood.

Nigel and Shirley won gold for Belgium in the 1984 World Ice Dance Championships.

SATANELLA - 16

Satanella was once a little girl as pretty as a bag of eels, but after a terrible accident with a prawn and a faulty wand, she was turned into a small dog.

- Likes - Anything that can't run as fast as she can.
- Dislikes - Anything that can run faster than she can.
- Hobbies - Biting things.
- Pets - A squeaky rubber human called Alan.*
- Favourite colour - Blurry fast-moving skin colour.

Satanella and Alan share a bonding moment.

---

* Alan was originally a council drains inspector who examined the Floods' drain a bit too closely. He is much happier now.

MERLINMARY - 15

No one is sure if Merlinmary is a boy or a girl. Even Merlinmary doesn't know. Mm's greatest talent is making electricity, which he/she does all the time.

- Likes - Thunder storms with lots of lightning.
- Dislikes - Gas.
- Hobbies - Putting lightbulbs in his/her ears and making them light up.
- Pets - Several cockroaches.*
- Favourite colour - Violent yellow.
- Favourite food - Fuse wire.

---

* Including Henri, a cockroach from Paris, who once won a stage in the Tour de France.

150

Although he looks as if he has been dead for a long time, Winchflat is the genius. He can outwit the fastest computer, count to eleven on his fingers and seventeen if he uses his toes too.

- Likes - Nerds, especially undead zombie nerds.
- Dislikes - Daylight.
- Hobbies - Chatrooms, or even better: chatdungeons.
- Pets - A very big dictionary called Trevor.
- Favourite colour - Darkness.
- Favourite food - Caffeine.

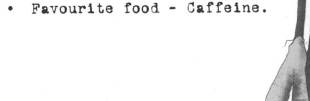

spo•rad•ic |spə'radik|
adjective
occurring at irregular intervals or only in a few places; scattered or isolated :
sporadic fighting broke out.

DERIVATIVES
spo•rad•i•cal•ly |-ik(ə)lē| adverb

ORIGIN late 17th cent.: via medieval Latin from Greek *sporadikos*, from *sporas, sporad- 'scattered'*; related to *speirein 'to sow.'*

Morbid and Silent are twins. To the
untrained eye, they are identical
twins but actually they are mirror
twins, which means they are identical
in every way except horizontally.
They are like the reflection of
each other in the mirror.
Morbid is right-handed,
Silent is left-handed -
except during the full
moon when they change
places. They communicate with
each other by telepathy.

- Likes - Silence.
- Dislikes - Not silence.
- Hobbies - Being silent.
- Pets - Each other.
- Favourite colour -
  Each other.
- Favourite food - Anything
  that doesn't make a noise
  when you eat it (except
  anything that ends with
  'mite', of course).

BETTY - 10

After six strange children, Mordonna decided she wanted a normal pretty little girl she could do cooking and sewing with. So she had Betty, who looks like a china doll. Unlike the rest of the 'children', who go to a special school in Patagonia, Betty goes to the ordinary school just down the road. She may look normal, but she still has awesome powers.

- Likes - Everything.
- Dislikes - Nothing.
- Hobbies - Embroidery, pressing flowers, washing up.
- Pets - a scraggy black cat called Vlad.
- Favourite colour - Pink.
- Favourite food - Fairy floss (leech flavour).

OTHER FAMILY PETS
Clarissa the dodo

Everyone knows that dodos are extinct. Humans discovered them in 1598 and in less than a hundred years managed to kill every single one. All except Clarissa, who is now 350 years old, although for 345 years of that time she was an egg, until Winchflat built his incredible iDodo Egg Hatching Machine.

Unfortunately they haven't managed to find another egg so Winchflat is now building an iDodo Hydrostatic Dodo Cloning Photocopier. One day we may see huge colonies of dodos roaming free, falling out of trees and walking into things.*

---

* *Dodos can't fly and their eyesight is rubbish, so it's not surprising they got wiped out.*

The night eels

I know there's nothing in the picture except black. That is the best I can do. Night eels live in total darkness and if even the slightest pinprick of light appears - like the faint neon light that tells you the battery on your mobile phone is nearly flat - they explode.

You only know they exist when you feel them, soft and wet and slippery, as they slide over your skin like wet velvet. If they like you, they'll wrap themselves around your face and stick their heads up one of your nostrils and their tails up the other. If you have three nostrils, they bring a friend. If they don't like you, they do the same thing but with electricity and more slime.

Winchflat tried to teach some night eels to sing, but the only noise they made was so depressing he couldn't bear to be with them for more than a few minutes a day.

HOW TO BUILD A Massive-Electric-Shock Dead-Person-iReviver

You will need:

- 1 dead person to revive.
- 10 dead people to practise on.
- 1 Krankovich 476B Portable Nuclear Reactor.
- 17 metres of big copper wire with bright red insulation.
- 1 colossal power source – eg. the sun or Merlinmary.
- Strong glue – sometimes the skull can burst open.
- Heavy-duty rubber gloves and boots.
- Goggles – in case of flying toes.

Blood spurting out of the dead person's nose is an unavoidable side-effect. Some people think this is a bonus.

The dead person's pyjamas nearly always catch fire. (Bloody good thing too.)

Granny Flood's Household Tips

How to get blood out of a white sheet
Pour lukewarm water through the stain into a china cup. Makes an excellent bedtime drink. Don't use boiling water as that will cook the blood, which is just disgusting.

How to get blood out of a sleeping human
Place your fangs on the jugular vein, press slowly and suck very quietly. Goes well with barbecued rat.

How to get blood out of a sleeping bank manager
Don't be ridiculous!

How to get blood into a sleeping bank manager
Why would you want to waste perfectly good blood?

How to make 'I Can't Believe It's Not Blood'

This recipe has been in Granny Flood's family for three hundred years and is a firm favourite at Christmas, when it is used instead of custard.

You will need:

- Two large bottles of tomato ketchup.
- 500 grams of black slugs.
- 3 tablespoons of black enamel paint.
- The end of your right thumb.

Put all the ingredients in a blender, cover your face and blend on high speed until smooth. Add chilli powder and saliva to taste.

Pour over Christmas pudding, small dogs or your own head, depending on the time of day.

Garnish with nose-hair clippings.

(Also goes well with lavatory lobsters.*)

---

* *A traditional Transylvania Waters delicacy, which has caused some very ferocious arguments over whether the best lavatory lobsters come from the men's or the ladies' lavatories.*

The Author file
COLIN THOMPSON

Colin Thompson
was born in
England but
finally had
the good sense
to move to
Australia in
1995.

As you can
see from the
picture on
the left, it
took him a
REALLY long
time to
write this
book.

- Born - Yes.
- Dislikes - Windows.
- Best thing that is small and black and shiny - my PSP.
- Pets - Dogs; Bonnie, Max and Charlie.
- Favourite colour - Silly question. I like blue for jeans but I wouldn't want to eat blue food (unless it was cake).
- Favourite food - Cherries.
- Best picture book I've done - How To Live Forever.
- Best novel I've written - How To Live Forever.

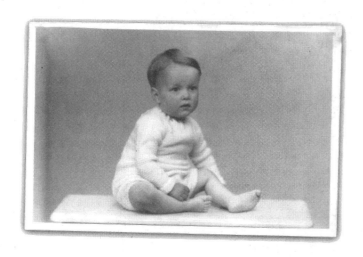

Promise me that, no matter what happens, no matter how desperate you feel, no matter who asks you, you will never, never, never, read this book.

Hidden behind the hundreds of secret doors in the museum, Peter will find an enchanted world, a cursed book and a terrible choice that could change his life for eternity.

How To Live FOREVER
Colin Thompson

AVAILABLE NOW AT ALL GOOD BOOKSTORES.

RANDOM HOUSE AUSTRALIA
www.randomhouse.com.au

The Floods' Family Tree

MERLIN ♥ **MORDONNA**
Wizard   Witch

Valla
Boy – 22

Satanella
Girl – 16

Merlinmary
Not sure – 15

Winchflat
Boy – 14

Morbid & Silent
Twin boys – 11

Betty
Girl – 10

Some Quicklime College teachers

Turn to page 204 for

The Quicklime College Teachers Files.

Your teachers

Look in ANY classroom.

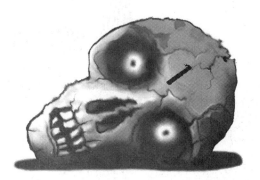

Most children start school when they're about five or six, even witch and wizard children. In fact, six of the seven Flood children started school at about the same age as you did. A particularly brilliant witch or wizard, however, may well start school before they are born.

Winchflat Flood, who is cleverer than a whole box of knives, began school eight months before he was born, when he was just a little tadpole. To help himself add things up more quickly, he grew an extra finger on each hand and three more toes on each foot, which is why he wears such big shoes. By the time he was born, he knew more stuff than almost anyone else in the whole world.

The children's father, Nerlin Flood, though quite clever, never went to school at all. Where Nerlin grew up in Transylvania Waters – a dark and mysterious country four weeks' ride by horseback beyond the furthest boundaries of Transylvania itself, turn left at the Valley of Doom and keep going until you pass through the Arches of Darkness – none of his relations had been to school. His family were Dirt People. They lived their whole lives in the drains beneath the city, cleaning the toilets from below and making sure everything always flowed away smoothly. The rest of the population looked down on them in every way, especially on Thursdays, when they would kneel on the pavement and shout rude words down the gratings into the drains just to make sure the Dirt People never got above themselves.

'Waste of good education, teaching them to read and write,' said King Quatorze.[1] 'I mean, they

---

[1] *The King's full title is eighteen pages long but here is a brief version: King-Nombre-Sept-À-Quatorze-Knees-And-Bumpsadaisy-The-Four-Hundred-And-Fourteenth-And-A-Half-Grand-Protector-Of-The-Haunted-Grapefruit-Keeper-Of-The-Holey-Pants-Guardian-Of-The-Square-Window-*

don't need to read anything to use a shovel and a toilet brush.'

'Exactly, Sire,' agreed his Chancellor. 'And besides, it's too dark down there to read anything anyway.'

On the other hand, Nerlin's wife, Mordonna, was a princess and had received the very best education Transylvania Waters could offer. Because she was the King's daughter, she didn't go to school with the common children. She had a special governess

---

Supreme-Cuddler-Of-The-Round-Widow-Prince-Of-Half-An-Hour-Before-Twilight-Kevin-King-Of-Cardboard-Keeper-Of-The-Dinner-Money-And-All-Who-Sail-In-Her-The-Ninth-Except-On-Tuesdays.

who lived in the palace and taught her everything she needed to know. However, because Mordonna was a princess and her governess, Claypit, was just a commoner, they were forbidden to talk to each other. This meant that, although it was always very peaceful in the schoolroom, actually learning anything was a bit difficult.

Like all clever people, Nerlin and Mordonna knew that you learn tons more useful stuff after you've left school than you do when you're there. In the years since they had eloped together and travelled the world pursued by King Quatorze's agents, Nerlin and Mordonna had gathered more knowledge and wisdom than most people ever do. Now they were brilliant at magic – and they were determined that their children would be even better. They would spare no expense when it came to their children's schooling.[2] This is why they sent their children to

---

[2] *Not that money is ever a problem for witches and wizards. If they can't find a way of stealing it, they just make it using a spell and some simple everyday ingredients like shoe polish and centipedes.*

Quicklime College – a special school for witches, wizards, goblins, elves, shamans and anyone else who can do magic, and the finest school of its kind in the world.

Their youngest child, Betty, is the exception. Betty goes to the normal human's school, Sunnyview Primary School, just down the road from where she lives at numbers 11 and 13 Acacia Avenue. Betty doesn't look like her brothers and sisters. She has blonde hair and no warts at all, and likes to do things that ordinary girls do, like baking cakes and knitting. Her cakes are normal cakes with no earwigs or cockroaches in them, and her knitting doesn't have the usual wizard's spiky thorns knitted into the cuffs.

Of course, being a witch, she can still do magic, though you can't tell by looking at her. And although she knows her parents would send her to Quicklime College with her brothers and sisters if she asked, Betty likes it at normal school – especially now that Dickie Dent is no longer there to pull her hair and tease her. She does get teased by some of the other girls for being a bit different, but it's nothing she can't handle with a bit of magic – 'pain and pimples', as she likes to call it.

Valla, the oldest Flood child, left Quicklime's with a first-class degree in blood and now goes

out to work at the blood-bank. This leaves the five remaining children: Satanella, Merlinmary, Winchflat, and the twins, Morbid and Silent. They all go to Quicklime's.

Quicklime's is hidden in a remote valley high in the mountains of distant Patagonia. It's so far from anywhere that almost no ordinary humans have ever been there or even know the valley exists. There are no roads or footpaths into the place and, as there are always security clouds spread evenly above it, it can't even be seen by satellite. It has never appeared on any maps at all.

The site was chosen because it was here that the first wizards arrived on Earth. It's a well-known fact that the original witches and wizards came from a far-off galaxy where spells and magic were something everyone could do. When they got bored, they'd get in a spaceship and fly off to another galaxy to scare and/or enchant the local population, who thought magic was magic.

Nerlin's ancestor,[3] Merlin Flood the Fifteenth, came to Earth to create a few legends for humans who, until then, had lived in caves and thought the best thing anyone could do was hit someone else on the head with a lump of wood – a belief that lots of humans still have. Unfortunately Merlin's spaceship had not been serviced properly before he left home and it crashed in a remote valley in Patagonia.

Merlin's first thought was, *Plank*, which was the rudest swear word he knew. His second thought

---

[3] *Nerlin's family hadn't always been Dirt People. Once they had ruled Transylvania Waters, but, as so often happens, treachery, revolution and badly fitting tights had led to their downfall.*

was, *This is a pretty cool valley*, and with the help of Big Magic, seven robots, a tape measure and some human peasants, he built Quicklime College.[4] This took a very long time and Quicklime's was opened for business seven hundred and fifty years ago, by which time there were quite a few witches and wizards living on Earth.

Work on Quicklime's was held up for ninety-nine years while Merlin went off to help the young King Arthur with his adventures and teach him handy household tips like how to sharpen a sword that some idiot has stuck in a rock and how to make a round table so none of his knights would feel like someone else had a more important seat than they did. What was left out of the history books was all the fights the knights had with each other because no one could tell whose seat they were sitting in. Someone would sit in the wrong place and eat someone else's dessert and

---

[4] *When the building was finished, Merlin turned the human peasants into upside-down blind cave fish, which still exist to this day. (This is true – when I was a boy my uncle had an upside-down blind cave fish in a tropical tank. It was pink, blind and swam upside down.)*

then the fight would start. The actual table still exists and is one of Quicklime College's most treasured possessions.

Quicklime's looks like a proper wizard school should look, with lots of very pointy towers and fancy gargles around the tops of the walls. Gargles are like gargoyles except they make a loud gargling noise all the time. The three hundred and sixty-five gargles at Quicklime's have been tuned to gargle in a slow eerie wail that can be heard from hundreds of miles away, which has led to the myth that there are giants in Patagonia, something humans believe to this day.

There are three hundred and sixty-five of everything at Quicklime's, except doors. There are only three hundred and sixty-four of them, which

means that, somewhere, there is a room without a door – though no one has ever managed to find it.

Quicklime College is more than a school, it's a way of life. And unlike normal school, you don't leave forever at the end of year 12. Quicklime's is a place you go back to your whole life. If you have a problem you can't solve, you can always find the answer at Quicklime's, either in the great library or in the brains of the professors, who have lived for thousands of years.

Very few Quicklime's students ever want to take a day off from school and, if they are sick, they usually stay in the school sick bay rather than go home. Matron has far more powers than the average witch and a list of incredible medicines as long as your arm. She even has medicines longer than your arm, ancient recipes from mythical ages lost in the mists of time, when dinosaurs roamed the world – which they actually still do in Quicklime College's valley.

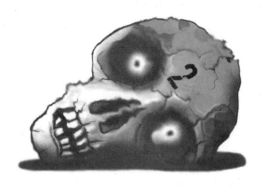

Monday morning, 8.01 am

'**S**orry we're late, kids,' said the driver as the wizard school bus arrived at 13 Acacia Avenue. 'Couldn't get the dragon started this morning. Must be the wet weather.'

Below the Floods' home at 11 and 13 Acacia Avenue was a vast network of cellars, and the bus stop was in one of these. It wasn't just the school bus that stopped there every day, but a whole range of witch and wizard transport. There were Shopping Specials that took all the mother witches to the UnderMall where they bought underwhere, extra-black eyeshadow and this season's new magical pointy objects. There were Sports Specials that took all the wizards to

intergalactic football games, and there were Holiday Specials that took the children to summer camp. All the buses were the same – not so much buses as dragons with seats and toilets, run by an interplanetary company called Blackhound. These buses travelled at a fantastic speed and there were express buses – dragons with seats and no toilets – that could travel at the speed of light. For technical reasons, which are too messy and complicated to explain, it is extremely

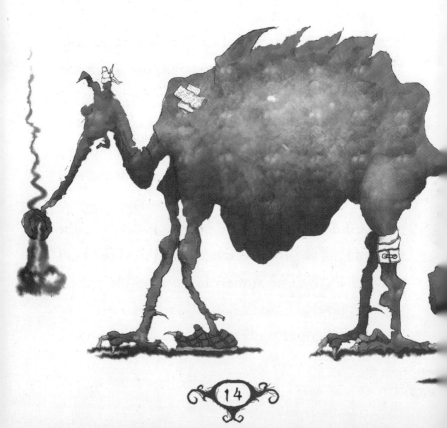

dangerous to go to the lavatory at the speed of light.

The dragon stood at the bus stop, with smoke trickling out of its nostrils. Its eyelids kept dropping shut as if it was about to fall back to sleep. It looked very old and tired, which it was. It had been taking children to Quicklime's for two hundred years and it wanted a rest. All it could think of was the school holidays when it could spend all day asleep in its cave. It should have retired years ago, but there was no one to take its place. Dragons have always been very misunderstood. Humans have never been able to see the poetry in them burning down the occasional village and carrying off beautiful women, and have persecuted them for centuries until dragons have sadly become an endangered species. The few remaining dragons are now protected by spells of invisibility so humans can never see them.

'Come on, children, we've got fifty-eight seconds to make up,' said the driver as the five Flood children climbed aboard. 'And no blood-letting in the back seats.'

Fifty-eight seconds might seem like less than a

minute, but when you travel as fast as a Blackhound school bus, that's all it takes to travel a few hundred miles.

The Flood children were the first on the bus each morning and always sat in the back row where they could see everything that was going on. Winchflat was head boy at Quicklime's, which meant he had the power to remove or seriously modify the head of any child who was naughty. He was so conscientious that he once removed his own head for twenty-four hours for accidentally tripping up a junior witch.

On a normal bus journey, it's nice to look out of the window as you travel along. On a dragon bus, all you see is blur, clouds, blur, and blur, but the journey is over so quickly there's no time to get bored. There's not even time to finish the homework you didn't do last night. Because a lot of wizard homework involves small unpleasant creatures, a fair bit of blood and slimy stuff, homework has been banned on school buses since the time an out-of-control intestine wrapped itself around the bus driver's eyes and made him crash into a volcano.

Morning Assembly
Headmaster: Professor Throat

Every morning the entire school gathered in the Grate Hall, which is not the Great Hall spelled in an old-fashioned way, but a huge room that has an enormous fireplace – the Great Grate – because it is very, very cold in the Patagonian Andes. At the opposite end of the hall, in the centre of the stage, sits King Arthur's round table.

Professor Throat stood in front of the round table and raised his hand. Gradually the children fell silent. Tame bats were put back in schoolbags. Extra heads were tucked inside shirts and light sabres were switched off. Even the school creep, Orkward

Warlock, managed to stop his right eye twitching for a few moments.

'As you all know,' the Professor began, 'in eight weeks time we have our annual sports day.'

Everyone cheered.

'Exactly,' Professor Throat continued. 'And we all know that sports day is the highlight of our school year, the only day when outsiders are invited to the school – your parents and siblings, former students dead and alive, and special guests from other worlds and dimensions. And this year, of course, is extra special because it is exactly seven hundred and fifty years since the school was opened by our glorious founder, Merlin Flood, in this beautiful valley, safe and secure in the high Patagonian Andes. So let's make this sports day the one that will go down in history.'

Everyone cheered, stamped their feet and threw stuff up in the air, including wizard hats, wands, toes, an elf called Nigel and several breakfasts.

'And now, all students please be silent for the school anthem,' said the Professor.

Unlike other schools, where everyone sings a really boring song while some dotty old lady plays on an out-of-tune piano, Quicklime's school anthem was sung in Braille. Everyone closed their eyes and ran their fingers over a card with the words embossed on it. It was the most peaceful three minutes and twenty-seven seconds of the day, just enough time for all the teachers to have a cup of tea and a biscuit.

It was hard that day to concentrate on the school anthem. The announcement about sports day was filling up everyone's head. Many children, including the Floods, had spent months preparing themselves with special training. Satanella had spent hours in the back garden of 13 Acacia Avenue chasing her tail round and round Queen Scratchrot's grave. So far she had never managed to catch it, which didn't really matter as there was no tail-chasing event in the school sports.

'Mind you,' she'd said to her brothers and sisters, 'as soon as I do catch my tail, I will petition for it to be included. I mean if they allow beach volleyball in the Olympics, they'd have to let tail chasing in.'

(Sport at Quicklime's is not like sport anywhere else. Here are a few of the best-loved events past and present:

- **Wizard Rules** – *Twenty-two players stand in the middle of a soccer field and watch as all the spectators kick a ball around the terraces. Sometimes the players get overexcited and throw things such as intestines and referees into the crowd.*

- **Gristleball** – *See the next chapter.*

- **The high jump** – *This was abandoned in 1873 after a small wizard, Obadiah Flood (distant relation), jumped up into the clouds and was never seen again. There is a small sect living in a cave near Mount Everest that is waiting for the day when Obadiah will return to Earth. They prophesy that this will be next Thursday just after lunch and he will reappear in Mexico. No one knows why they are waiting in the Himalayas.*

- **The long jump** – *Because this event took too long, it has been replaced by the short jump. The school record is 0.003 seconds.*

- **Cross country** – *In 1994, the school made Belgium so cross that everyone at Quicklime's had to wear a T-shirt for the rest of the year that said: 'Belgium is not at all boring. It is a really, really interesting place.'*

- **The pole vault** – *Temporarily cancelled because*

there is no more room in the vault and Poland has lodged a complaint with the United Nations.

- **Three-legged race** – *Teams are made up of families. Where there are more than two children, like in the Flood family, they are all tied together and have to leave some of their legs in the changing room. Where there is only one child, they are allowed to grow an extra leg for the day. There is always a protest about this race from the Millipedes – a family of witches and wizards from a damp ditch in Tristan da Cuhna – who claim the whole race is 'leggist'.*

- **Long distance cricket** – *You will probably find it hard to believe but long distance cricket is actually slower and even more boring than normal cricket. One wicket is on the school playing field and the other wicket is thousands of kilometres away in the back yard of number 7, The Street, St Kilda.*[5]

---

[5] *A very remote island off the west coast of the Outer Hebrides, which is off the north-west coast of Scotland.*

23

Top score for a three-day match is Quicklime College 3, Scotland 0.)

After the school anthem, other teachers stood up one by one with various announcements: things that had been lost – the usual iPods, fountain pens and fingers; and things that had been found – usually nothing because the school was kept very clean and tidy by someone we shall meet later.

And as it was the first Assembly of term, there was a report of the past holiday's great achievements by students and ex-students. The highlight that holiday had been Winchflat Flood's creation of a volcano right at the North Pole.

'Talk about global warming!' said Professor Throat to hoots of laughter.

'Well, I thought that was what they wanted,' said Winchflat. 'What with so many humans walking around whingeing about how cold they were.'

Finally, Assembly was dismissed and everyone went off to their classes. Classes at Quicklime's are different from those at other schools. Apart from the

subjects being much more interesting, children of different ages are often in the same class. Quicklime College knows that you don't get more clever as you get older. You're as clever when you die as you are on the day you're born. The only difference is that you know more stuff.

Even better, the school doesn't make anyone go to any lessons they find boring – which is a bit like a Steiner school, except that at Quicklime's everyone actually learns to read and write. So, if you are really keen on something like genetic engineering, you can go to every single Genetic Engineering class each week no matter what age you are. And if you think that maths is boring, which of course it is, you don't have to go to any Maths classes. The only rule is that you have to go to four classes every day.

The Flood twins, Morbid and Silent, went off to study Invisibility. Satanella trotted off to her Special Breeds class.

Winchflat, who was brilliant at everything, shook a little bag with all the lessons written on different tiles, like Scrabble, and picked out the class

he would go to first. His favourite class was Genetic Engineering, so to make sure he went to that class more often than the others, he had twenty-three tiles with 'Genetic Engineering' written on them and only one each for the other subjects.

And Merlinmary went off to play Gristleball.

Lesson: Sport with Pain
Teacher: Radius Leg

'Today, children, we will enjoy the pain that great sport can bring,' said Radius Leg. 'I don't mean the pain caused by the screaming boredom of watching a normal human soccer match or the pain of trying to stay awake during a normal human cricket match. Nor do I mean the mild physical pain of playing cricket with hand grenades. I mean the sheer bone-breaking, skin-tearing, blood-squirting, bubonic-plague-ridden joy of Quicklime College's own special game: Gristleball.'

The thirty-nine children in the class were standing at the top of the Gristleball field as the

school's sports teacher addressed them. They were all raring to go because, like all lessons at Quicklime's, you didn't have to go to Gristleball classes unless you wanted to. The only student who had no choice was Orkward Warlock. Orkward spent his entire life at the school, including holidays, weekends, half-term and even Christmas Day, and because he was a naturally lazy boy, Professor Throat had decided he should play Gristleball to get some exercise.

Unlike other sports, there were no different leagues for boys and girls. In fact, when the players were dressed in their protective clothing, you couldn't tell who was a boy and who was a girl.

Gristleball was not played on the normal school playing field. Because of the frequent accidents, it had its own special place away from the rest of the school in a one-hundred-metre deep three-sided pit carved into the rock. This helped to muffle the sounds of agony that accompanied every game. At the bottom of the pit sat the playing field. There was no soft girly grass and mud down here, just smooth slippery marble. On each side of the field there was a goal similar in shape and size to a football goal, except the goals were alive and could change size. Radius Leg and the players were lowered into the Gristleball pit in a wicker basket.

'Right,' said Radius Leg. 'Misery House side one, Leech House side two, and Gored House side three.'

Orkward Warlock, who was in Misery House, took up his usual position of creeping off the field and hiding in the toilets, which were in a little cave near one of the corners. He always pretended he was in there in case the gristleball came flying through the window, but everyone knew he was just scared.

Radius Leg moved to the boundary and blew his whistle. In the centre of the triangle, the ground began to shake. The marble cracked from side to side, rose up and suddenly burst open as the ballworm reared up out of its tunnel. It tipped its head back, heaved, opened its mouth wide and spat a massive ball of slimy gristle embedded with nails into the air. As the ball shot up into the clouds, the ballworm slid back into its burrow, pulling the rocks and marble

back down behind it. The players stood looking up into the sky, waiting for the gristleball to reappear.

Three minutes went by as the gristleball hovered above the clouds, waiting for the moment when the players would drop their concentration for a split second.

Merlinmary Flood loved Gristleball. Round the walls of her bedroom in Acacia Avenue she had photographs of all the greatest teams and players Quicklime's had ever produced. If it had been up to her, she would have played Gristleball every day, but it was only played once a week to allow the players time to re-grow the bits of their bodies that had broken off during the game. With her incredibly thick hair crackling with electricity, she was the only player in the history of the school who had played the game

without protective clothing. Those few minutes when the ball hid in the clouds were the most exciting moments of her life. The anticipation was almost too much to bear and it was all Merlinmary could do not to give herself a serious electric shock.

The seconds ticked by as the ball hovered. The seconds became another minute and still the gristleball waited. And then, at the very moment when the players least expected it, it came screaming down, heating up as it did so until it was glowing red. If a team was ready and in the right place, they grabbed the gristleball in their asbestos gloves and threw it into the nearest goal.

If it was their own goal they got ten points. If it was either of the other two goals they scored five. For every other player the ball crashed into, seven points were added. If it hit Radius Leg and threw him against the boundary wall, the team got fifteen points plus one extra point for each broken rib.

That day, the ball flew straight down towards Merlinmary, but she was ready. She grabbed it and, ignoring the smell of her own fur beginning to burn,

she spun round in a blur of sparks and fire before hurling it with an almighty scream. It knocked three players to the ground, smashed through the lavatory window and threw Orkward Warlock down into the toilet bowl with such force that the entire thing shattered, leaving him sitting in a pool of water with the wooden toilet seat around his neck like a huge collar.

'Goatface pig bottom!!' he screamed through his pain as the ball shot back through the window towards the opposite side of the field. For as long as

he could remember, Orkward Warlock had hated the Floods. Every day there was something else they did that made him hate them more.

Merlinmary's throw shot through all three goals before hovering just out of reach in one of the corners of the playing pit while the gristleball regained its strength. Her score was forty-one points, though when it was later discovered what had happened to Orkward Warlock another twenty-seven points and a gold star were added – seven for hitting Orkward and a special referee's bonus of twenty for smashing the toilet, which no one had ever done before. The fact that he had been the source of Merlinmary getting anothet twenty-seven points made Orkward hate the Floods even more.

The game ended when the gristleball ran out of energy. It collapsed in the corner panting for breath until Radius Leg gave it a drink of water and summoned the ballworm to take it back to its nest.

The highest score ever for a single throw had been four years before, when Valla Flood, in his final game before leaving school, had thrown the

gristleball through his own goal with such force that it had thrown Radius Leg against the wall and broken nine of his ribs before bouncing back across the field seventeen times through all three goals and finally hitting Radius Leg a second time, breaking both of his legs. The score was one hundred and eighty-seven points, more than double the previous record. It had earned Valla a lifetime honour award, fifty out of ten and a whole bucket of gold stars.

'They don't make gristle like that any more,' Radius Leg would say proudly, stroking his scars as he remembered that wonderful day.

Orkward Warlock hated everyone. He hated his parents. He hated his sister Primrose, who was disgustingly nice, and he hated all the other relations he assumed he had but had never met. He hated his teachers and every other person he knew or read about or saw on TV. Sometimes, for practice, he even hated himself, and pretty well everyone hated him too.

But Orkward Warlock had one hate that was deeper than all his other hates. It was so dark and deep that it had no end, like the lake in Scotland where the Loch Ness Monster lives. This hate was bigger than all Orkward's other hates added together and multiplied by twelve plus seven.

The thing that Orkward Warlock hated more than anything in the whole universe was the Floods.

Orkward Warlock was one of the twenty-seven boarders at Quicklime's. The boarders were usually children who lived too far away to be able to come to school by bus each day. The fleet of wizard buses that took the children to and from school covered the entire globe. There was even one very small witch – Felicia McThursday – who came from a lighthouse on a remote rock fifty kilometres past Iceland. The children who boarded at Quicklime's came from even further away, from other galaxies and parallel universes.

All except Orkward. He was the only boarder who actually came from Earth, and *he* was a boarder because his parents couldn't stand to have him at home, not even during the holidays. He had spent every single day of his life since the age of three days at Quicklime's. In the holidays, when everyone, including his sister Primrose and most of the teachers, went home, Orkward stayed behind with Matron, Doorlock the handyman, George Shrub the

mandrake gardener and Narled, a strange creature, half man, half suitcase, who spent the whole time picking things up and taking them somewhere.

Over the years, several children and teachers had invited Orkward to come and stay with them in the holidays, but to everyone's relief he had always refused.

'I think my parents are coming to take me to Tahiti,' he would say, but everyone knew it wasn't true.

Because Orkward was at school all the time, Professor Throat had given him his own room up in one of the seven-sided turrets. It was there, in the darkness, where even spiders were afraid to go, that Orkward practised hating. Around the walls of the room, he had photographs of everyone – every student, every teacher and all the other staff – and

into these photographs he stuck pins and knives and knitting needles. Everyone knew he was doing this and wore an amulet issued by Matron that protected them against the magic.[6]

---

[6] *Radius Leg chose not to wear his amulet as he liked the sudden unexpected searing bolt of agony when Orkward stuck a needle in his photo. When Orkward found out about this, he immediately stopped doing it.*

Sticking pins into pictures of the Floods wasn't enough for Orkward. It didn't begin to cover the hatred that he felt for them. They had everything. They had brothers and sisters to play with and parents who loved them, and they all seemed to like each other. They even did smiling,[7] and their mother, Mordonna, was one of the most famous witches that had ever existed. Her beauty was legendary across the galaxies. Her photo was pinned up in cafes and bars in every one of the fifteen parallel universes. Orkward didn't even know what his own mother looked like. All he could remember about her was a blurry face close to his and a voice saying, 'Take it away, it's the ugliest thing I've ever seen.'

Nerlin, the Floods' father, as well as being a direct descendant of Merlin Flood the Fifteenth, was in *The Hemlock Book of Records* as the owner of the world's hairiest wart in the most embarrassing place. Everyone at Quicklime's thought Nerlin was a

---

[7] *Orkward had tried smiling once but his mirror had laughed at him and the whole thing had made both him and the mirror sick for a week.*

legend – even though he'd never attended the school. Orkward had no memory of his own father and no one had ever spoken of him, not even Primrose.

Primrose never spoke to Orkward about anything. It had come as a complete surprise to both of them to discover, after Primrose had been at Quicklime's for four years, that they were actually brother and sister. Orkward was one of those boys who thought girls were gross and didn't want anything to do with her. Primrose, like almost everyone at Quicklime's, thought Orkward was vile and wanted as few people as possible to know she was related to him. Orkward had tried a couple of times to befriend his sister so he could find out about their parents, but his attempts at friendship were a bit like a crocodile

trying to make friends with your leg. He just didn't know how to do normal things like smiling or being nice. In the end Primrose told him they were not related and that he had been adopted. It wasn't true, but at least it meant he stopped bothering her.

When no one was watching or listening, Orkward would lie in bed in the darkness and nearly allow himself to cry. He would imagine a gigantic white dragon arriving in the valley with the greatest wizard in creation riding on its back, a wizard who was king of all the other wizards, a wizard who had arrived for one reason and one reason only – to claim his long-lost son, Orkward Warlock.

The truth was not so wonderful. Orkward Warlock's father was a milkman, an ordinary middle-aged balding human with no magical powers and a small moustache that he called Gerald. Orkward's mother, who was a genuine witch, had only married him because she was addicted to milk and couldn't afford the fifty litres a day she needed to drink and bathe in to keep her skin glowing white.

Orkward had only two friends. One was an

innocent boy known as The Toad, who spent many hours under Orkward's bed cuddling Orkward's dirty socks. The other was a magic mirror, but that didn't really like him or tell him what he wanted to hear.

'Mirror, Mirror on the wall,' Orkward would say, 'who is the cleverest boy of all?'

'Winchflat Flood,' The Mirror would reply. 'Why do you keep asking me? You, like, totally know the answer, idiot.'

'You are, Orkward,' The Toad would call out from under the bed. But Orkward would always get so angry he would take The Mirror off the wall and stick it under the bed with The Toad.

'Mirror, Mirror on the floor,' Orkward would say, 'who has the most evil eyes?'

'Merlinmary Flood,' The Mirror replied.

'You do,' squeaked The Toad as Orkward threw a well-aimed boot under the bed.

Whatever Orkward asked The Mirror, the answer was always one of the Floods.

'Enough with the Floods already!' screamed Orkward as his brain contorted itself in rabid anger.

'I need a plan,' he said, trying to calm himself down. 'A plan to finish the Floods off once and for all.'

'Sports day,' whimpered The Toad.

'Shut up, slug pus,' sneered Orkward and threw another boot under the bed. 'Don't you need to go somewhere and shed skin?'

'You could get them on sports day,' said The Toad, crawling out to get Matron's special bruise ointment, which he always kept close by since he'd become friends with Orkward. 'It's the only day when they're all together at the same time, and it would be really dramatic and worthy of your great evil.'

'Shut up, shut up, shut up!' shouted Orkward, stamping his foot on the tube of bruise ointment. He had forgotten that he'd thrown both his boots at The Toad, and the purple ointment began to soak through his socks and dissolve his toenails.

The Toad started to lick Orkward's toes clean. The Toad lived with a terrible conflict going on inside his head. Basically he was a sweet kind child, but because he was a toad, not many people wanted to be his friend. No one at all wanted to be

45

Orkward Warlock's friend, so when The Toad came along, Orkward took him under his evil wing. The trouble was, there was no place for sweet and kind in Orkward's world so The Toad had to pretend to be nasty and mean like Orkward.

'Hold on,' Orkward said. 'Even though you are fifty million degrees more stupid than an amoeba, that is actually a brilliant idea. Sports day is the highlight of the year. I will make this one the sports day to end all sports days, the ultimate sports day, the sports day people will remember forever, when all the Floods will die in one magnificent, er, skull-shattering, um … something or other.'

'YES!' cried The Toad.

'No you won't,' said The Mirror glumly from under the bed. 'You'll totally stuff it up. You always, like, do.'

'One more crack from you,' Orkward snapped, 'and you'll get a million cracks with a hammer.'

'Was that meant to be, like, a joke?' said The Mirror.

'I don't do jokes,' said Orkward.

Lesson: Invisibility
Teacher: Prebender Glorious

Prebender Glorious stood in front of the class with his usual Monday morning thought crashing against the inside of his skull. The thought was: *I wish I was anywhere but here.*[8]

Prebender Glorious taught Invisibility and he taught it very badly. He himself had a habit of

---

[8] *That was the abbreviated thought and all Prebender Glorious had time for. The full thought was:* I wish I was anywhere but here, doing any job but this, preferably a job that never brought me within two miles of anyone under twenty-five. What have I done to deserve this? Did I lock the back door when I left the house? I don't have a back door. I don't even have a house! *And so on for forty-three pages.*

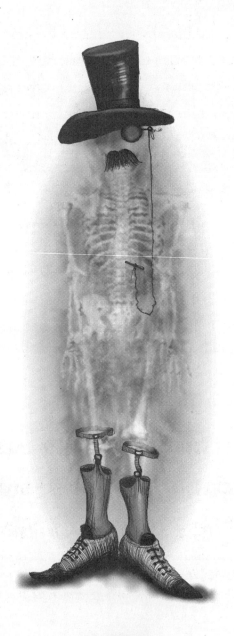

vanishing without any warning and reappearing just as suddenly.[9] It was a talent or curse he had been born with, and he had no control over it. Over the years it had brought him a lot of embarrassment, excitement, six months in prison, several million dollars and a string of failed love affairs. Sometimes just bits of him would disappear, which made going to the toilet and eating very difficult or very hilarious, depending on where you were standing.

His students, on the other hand, had mastered invisibility on their first day in the class, and now made his life hell. He sighed and took out the class register to mark everyone off.

'Portia Appleby?' There was a small pop and one of the students disappeared.

There are three children here, but they are invisible.

While Prebender Glorious looked around for Portia, Orkward Warlock leaned forward and whispered to Morbid and Silent Flood, 'You're all going to die.'

The twins ignored him. They were used to Orkward's snide remarks and knew he was all talk.

'Portia Appleby? Where's Portia?' Prebender Glorious asked.

'Right here, sir,' said Portia, appearing out of thin air.

'But I'm not,' said Bypass Noble, vanishing.

'Now, look, come on, everyone, play fair,' Prebender Glorious pleaded, on the verge of tears.

'But we're just doing what you've been teaching us,' said Portia and the whole class vanished, except Howard Tiny, who was horribly good and didn't count. Actually he did count, really well, but never got past ninety-nine before someone stuffed something in his mouth, because as well as being horribly good, he was also horribly boring.

'Oh God, Tiny, why do they always vanish and leave me with you?'

'I don't know, sir. Would you like me to do some counting?'

'No, it's all right, thank you,' said Prebender Glorious. 'You just sit there and practise your invisibility. Try and make your mouth vanish.'

'Okay, sir. Can I count quietly? It helps me concentrate.'

'If you must.'

'One, two, three, four ...'

Orkward Warlock could do invisibility but he wasn't very good at it. When you are really good at it, you can see everyone else who is invisible at the same time as you are. Orkward Warlock couldn't. All he could see when the class vanished was Prebender Glorious and Howard Tiny. For all he knew, everyone else had left the room.

'Going to kill us, are you?' Morbid Flood whispered in his left ear, while Silent blew hot breath in his right. 'We're really scared,' the voice added. 'Not!'

Two very large invisible books whacked Orkward on either side of his head. For a split second

he became visible again before collapsing on the floor with his breakfast coming out of his nose.

'Nose blister scumbags!' he shouted. 'I really am going to kill you.'

He staggered to his feet and kicked Howard Tiny, who started to cry. Orkward disappeared again before he could get into trouble.

The Monday morning thought beat even harder inside Prebender Glorious's head.

'Eighty-seven, eighty-eight, eighty-nine ...' Howard sobbed.

Something snapped inside Prebender. It was his third rib disappearing. He began to wish he could have a heart attack. It would be less stressful than teaching this lot, but he knew that even if he died he would still have to teach the Invisibility class. Being dead, which several other teachers were, just meant the school could stop paying your wages. It also looked very good in the school brochure.

'Ninety-five, ninety-six, ninety-sevvv ...' said Howard as Orkward Warlock's invisible hand stuffed a sock in his mouth.

There were two words guaranteed to make the students visible again and Prebender Glorious said them.

'Sports day.'

The entire class reappeared and sat quietly in their seats.

'As you all know, invisibility is totally absent from sports day,' he began. 'I mean, have we ever seen any invisible sports? No we haven't, and I for one think that it's very unfair. I petitioned the board of governors. I've even threatened to take the whole thing to the Wizard Rights Commission, and I am delighted to say that this year we will have invisibility on sports days. It will be there for all to not see.'

The class cheered with delight. Maybe they had misjudged poor old Prebender Glorious.

'What invisible events will there be, sir?' asked Bypass Noble.

'Throwing the javelin, for one,' said Prebender Glorious.

'So what exactly will be invisible?' asked Morbid. 'Us or the javelin?'

'Both.'

'Wow. So how will anyone know how far the javelin's gone or even where it's gone?' said Portia Appleby.

'By the bloodstains on the grass,' Prebender Glorious explained.

'I like it,' said Orkward Warlock. 'Can we practise on each other?'

'No, Orkward, you cannot. Now we will practise our invisible maths for the rest of the lesson.'

Everyone except Howard vanished again but, as the end-of-lesson bell rang, they all reappeared.

'Right, children, homework ...' Prebender Glorious began to say, but they all vanished again. 'Okay, we'll ... we'll skip homework again. Class dismissed.'

At which point the whole class reappeared and ran out of the room, except Howard Tiny, who was lying under his desk going purple as he tried to pull the sock out of his mouth, which would have been a lot easier if his foot hadn't still been inside it. Prebender rolled his eyes and went to help him, the Monday morning thought crashing around his skull with the force of a jackhammer.

From a distance, and especially when he was sitting still, Narled looked exactly like a very old suitcase. Up close you could see he had two little stubby legs at the front, two wheels at the back and a pair of arms. He appeared to have neither eyes, nor ears, nor a mouth. Where his mouth should have been was a wide leather flap that closed with a zip. Everyone assumed that Narled was once a human who had been changed into a suitcase by a spell that had been interrupted or put on him by some particularly cruel wizard, but despite all the teachers' attempts, no amount of magic had been able to undo the spell.

All day long Narled trundled round Quicklime's picking up things. Not just rubbish, but anything

that wasn't nailed down. He scooped it up with one hand, stuck it into his mouth and closed his zip. No one knew where he took all the stuff he collected, but if you left anything lying around for more than a few minutes, Narled would appear and take it away. He seemed to arrive from nowhere, and he had a strange way of being able to give people the slip. He would turn a corner into a dead end, but when you turned after him, he had vanished. There were rumours that he had a vast treasure house somewhere in the valley where he'd stashed all the things he had collected over the past six hundred years, but no one had ever found it.

'He must have stuff that's worth a fortune,' said Orkward Warlock. 'Gold and jewels and things that have become really valuable just because they're so old.'

'Shall I follow him?' said The Toad.

'Better people than you have tried,' sneered Orkward. 'In fact, anyone who's tried was better than you, you piece of dehydrated camel snot.'

The Toad worshipped Orkward, no matter how vile he was to him. Just the fact that Orkward spoke to him made The Toad happy. He looked up adoringly at Orkward, which made the boy so angry he did the yellow oozing pimple spell all over The Toad's face. This only made The Toad even happier.

'Anyway,' said Orkward, 'we need to work out a way to kill the Floods on sports day.'

'Poison,' said The Toad.

'They're wizards, idiot. Poison doesn't work on wizards.'

'Concrete,' said The Toad.

'Shut up. Or would you like me to throw something hard and smelly at you?' said Orkward.

'Ooh yes,' cried The Toad. 'Can I have the big brick? Please, go on, go on, please, please …'

'Paper. Get me paper and a pen,' Orkward ordered. 'We are going to write down every single possible way you can kill a bunch of wizards.'

An hour later the paper looked like this:

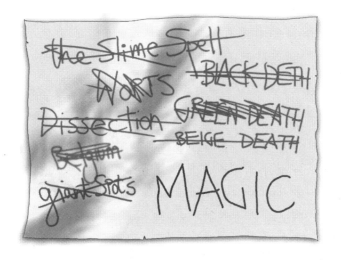

'I know,' said The Toad. 'You need a big explosion.'

'Shut up, shut up, shut up!' shouted Orkward, stamping his foot on The Toad's lunch. 'Actually,' he added, as The Toad licked bits of wasp sandwich off

the bottom of Orkward's shoes, 'even though you are fifty billion degrees more stupid than a fly-speck, that is a brilliant idea.'

'I know how to make explosions,' said The Toad. 'My father owns the biggest firework factory in the world and I know how to make gunpowder. I blew up the toilets when I was in kindy. That's why Professor Throat made me into a toad.'

'You mean you're a real toad?' said Orkward. 'I thought you were just a really ugly boy. Yuk, a real toad, that's gross.'

'Well, I'm not one hundred per cent toad,' said The Toad. 'Each year I get a bit less toady and a bit more humany, unless I do something really bad again. Now I'm seventy per cent toad. If I'm good for the next seven years I'll be all human again.'

'You colour-blind septic-tank bog rat,' said Orkward suddenly, and kicked The Toad under the bed. 'I was sitting on those toilets when you blew them up! I couldn't sit down for two months.'

Lesson: Special Breeds

Teacher: Miss Phyllis

The Toad placed a lily pad on his seat, sat on it and waited for the class to begin. It was his favourite lesson of the week: 'Flies and Their Place in Everyday Life'. Being a toad, he knew exactly where a fly's place was. It was inside his stomach. You might think there's not much to learn about eating flies, but if you've ever swallowed a wasp you'll know it's not that simple.

Most of the other class members were less interested in today's lesson. The dogs, for example, thought flies were just a nuisance that kept trying to eat their bones and sniff their bottoms. The cats

simply thought flies were beneath contempt.[10]

The Special Breeds class at Quicklime's was for those children who, for one reason or another, had been turned into animals. Because there was such a wide variety of animals it wasn't so much about learning things as about keeping the children occupied all day. The classes were held in one of the outbuildings because the smell could get a bit overpowering at times – especially by Friday, when the sawdust hadn't been changed all week.

Some children, like The Toad, had been turned into animals as a punishment. Lucretia De Lager had bitten the

---

[10] *Actually cats are dreadful snobs and think all other creatures are beneath contempt.*

head off the sugar plum fairy and eaten it. She had
been turned into a cat. Squire Nutkin had been
changed into a squirrel simply because he had such
an awful name.[11] Brian Lowflush had been turned
into a bird of paradise as a reward, and others, like
Satanella Flood, who was a small black dog, had been
changed by accident.[12]

Everything was different in the Special Breeds
class. Animals know that there are a million more
interesting, exciting and useful things than learning

---

[11] *No one ever said it was easy being a wizard.*

[12] *Mordonna kept offering to turn Satanella back into a little
girl, but she had decided life was more fun as a dog. 'Of course,
if I fall in love with a handsome wizard I'll probably want to
change back,' she said. 'But on the other hand I might fall in
love with a whippet.'*

how to add numbers up.[13] Dog numbers are easy. There are only two numbers for them: 'some' and 'none'. And that's two more numbers than snails need. Of course, the teachers tried to teach the animal-kids things they thought would be useful, but statements like 'Hello, children, today we are going to learn about French verbs' were usually greeted with replies like 'Grrrr' or 'Hiss' or 'Bark off'.

In the end, they reached a compromise, which basically meant no boring stuff like Maths and Belgian and History, and lots of very interesting stuff like eating flies and spiders, catching red rubber balls and chasing small defenceless animals. Each day focused on the interests of a different type of animal and Tuesday, The Toad's favourite, was amphibians day. The favourite activity that day was playing with the dress-up box. Everyone enjoyed that, though they got annoyed when the octopus kept taking all the high-heeled shoes.

'Right, children, spider juggling,' said Miss

---

[13] *Except the Millipede family, who are obsessed with numbers and spend all day counting their legs.*

Phyllis. 'Now we all know what happened last week when Nigel tried to juggle six tarantulas, and I'm happy to tell you that he is now out of the coma. So this week we are going to start off by juggling ants.'

The only child who enjoyed this was Kevin Flamboyard, who had been turned into an anteater by an ant he had eaten who was a leprechaun in disguise and not an ant at all. Kevin flicked his tongue round the classroom and swallowed every single ant.

'Okay, children, moving on,' said Miss Phyllis. 'Sports day is coming up and, as you know, the Special Breeds class always puts on an event. Last year we did underwater juggling, though unfortunately we did lose a few students like Norma Jean Gorgeous the butterfly. This year we need to come up with something safe that the whole class can be in without anyone drowning or exploding. Any ideas?'

'Tail chasing,' said Satanella.

'Some of us haven't got tails,' said The Toad.

'Well, you could all chase mine,' said Satanella.

'It's an idea,' said Miss Phyllis.

'How about tying a time bomb to her tail,'

suggested one of the rats, 'and if we don't catch it in time, it explodes?'

Satanella reminded the rat what small dogs could do to rats. In the end it was agreed that they would chase Satanella's tail around the running track but there would be no time bombs involved.

'How about a firework?' said the rat.

'Everyone has their price,' said Orkward, 'even a crappy old suitcase.'

'But Narled can't hear you,' said The Toad.

'I think he can,' said Orkward. 'You just watch him closely. Don't forget that I'm here in the holidays when there's no one around. I've seen him. I think he can hear and I think he can see.'

Orkward put on his silent shoes and went down into the quadrangle, where he hid behind a small tree and waited. The quadrangle was the central point of Quicklime's. Almost everyone in the entire school passed through one of its thirteen arches at some time of the day or night, including Narled.

Sure enough, fifteen minutes later, the tell-tale

squeak of his little wooden wheels told Orkward he was coming. The creature entered the quadrangle from the ninth arch, criss-crossed the grass and cobbles, picking up odd bits of rubbish and another forgotten iPod, and left through the seventh arch. Orkward followed him, his silent shoes completely silent even when he trod on a sheet of bubble-wrap containing a squeaky rubber bone.[14]

But Orkward knew that Narled knew he was there. He didn't know how, and the creature certainly gave no sign that he was aware of Orkward following him, but he knew. Orkward knew and he knew that Narled knew he knew and that Narled knew he knew he knew.

Narled went through the main gate, across the bridge over the black moat, where a class of year 5 students were being taught Underwater Japanese, and turned left along the dirt track that led down into the bottom of the valley. As he rounded a corner, he turned suddenly and slipped between two bushes.

---

[14] *Which Narled had strangely failed to pick up.*

But Orkward had seen him and followed into the dark forest that surrounded the school. When they had gone a few hundred metres into the gloom, the path ended in a small clearing and Narled stopped.

'I need your help,' Orkward said. 'I'll make it worth your while.'

Narled turned and faced the boy.

'So you *can* hear me,' said Orkward.

Narled sat back on his wheels and tilted his handle to one side. Orkward thought he saw the sides of the suitcase move slowly in and out as if Narled was breathing. He looked old and tired, as only a very well-travelled suitcase can look.

'If you help me,' said Orkward, 'I'll polish you.'

Narled's handle quivered.

'I'll polish you with the finest linseed oil and beeswax,' Orkward continued.

Narled's whole body quivered and gave a great sigh.

'All you have to do is carry a small box from A to B and leave it there,' said Orkward. 'You could do that, couldn't you?'

Narled frowned, which meant the bit of leather above his zip wrinkled a bit. He began to open his zip as if to speak, but then closed it again.

'I'll tell you what,' said Orkward. 'Just to show I mean it, I'll meet you here tomorrow and I'll bring the polish and a very soft black velvet cloth.'

Narled un-frowned, quivered, and turned away. The dark forest opened its branches and Narled trundled off into the darkness. Orkward tried to follow him, but the branches locked together again, barring his way. Although he wanted to go after Narled, he was, like all bullies, a terrible coward and was quite relieved that he could go no further.

'I'll take that as a yes then,' he said and hurried back to the college.

'Where the hell am I going to get some linseed oil and beeswax polish?' said Orkward, pacing up and down in his room.

'Matron's got some,' said The Toad, hopping back and forth out of Orkward's way. 'She put it on my back when I got sunburnt.'

'Well, go and get it, you pee bottle.'

'She won't just hand it over,' said The Toad. 'She said it's priceless, Matron's Enchanted Wax, been in her family for generations, the same magical

71

self-filling tin. It was given to her great-great-great-great-great-great-great-great-grandmother by Merlin himself to polish King Arthur's round table.'

'Well, go and steal it then, twit brain,' Orkward ordered.

'I don't know where she keeps it.'

'Well, go out and get sunburnt again.'

'But sunshine is banished here. You know that,' whimpered The Toad. 'When I got burnt before, it was that afternoon when He Who Must Not Be Talked About took away the clouds.'

'He Who Must Not Be Talked About?' said Orkward. 'Who the hell's He Who Must Not Be Talked About?'

'I don't know, no one ever talks about him.'

'I think you just made him up,' said Orkward, furious that he had never heard of someone so evil even his name couldn't be spoken, and so clever he could steal all the clouds. 'I've never heard of him.'

'That's because no one ever talks about him,' The Toad tried to explain.

'You just did,' said Orkward. 'Oh well, we'll just

have to improvise. Where's my massively powerful flame gun?'

'Wh-wh-what do you want it for?' asked The Toad, thinking it might be a good time to find a cold wet stone to crawl under.

'Well, if the sun won't burn you, I'll have to.'

'I'd rather you didn't,' said The Toad.

'Don't be such a baby, it won't hurt.'

'Yes it will.'

'Oh yes, so it will,' said Orkward. 'But it won't hurt *me*.'

There was a big flash, a loud scream of pain and a rather pleasant smell of braised toad.

As he carried the whimpering creature to sick bay, Orkward whispered, 'Now listen, you little slimeball. Matron will ask you how this happened and when she finds out it was me, she'll come looking for me. That's when you grab the polish and take it to our secret place, where I'll be waiting.'

'But …' The Toad began.

'Fail and I'll kill you,' said Orkward, dropping The Toad at the sick bay door and backing away.

'Succeed and you'll get a big reward.'

'Reward? Wow, what reward?'

'I won't kill you.'

Lesson: Genetic Engineering

Teacher: Doctor Mordant

Doctor Mordant stood in front of the class while his students settled into their seats. Genetic engineering was one of the most popular classes at Quicklime's, not just because the idea of creating new and exciting lifeforms was a lot more fun than French or History, but also because of Doctor Mordant himself. Doctor Mordant was so devoted to his subject that he constantly practised his skill on his own body. He currently had three arms, two heads and a chicken's foot, though, as everyone knew, this could change at a moment's notice.

For example, this Tuesday there was something

beginning to grow out of one of his heads that could only be described as broccoli.

'Right, class, homework,' said Doctor Mordant's left head. 'How did you all get on? Did you produce something?'

Most of the children nodded and held up their hands to be first to show their results.

'Excellent,' said Doctor Mordant's right head. 'Let us re-cap. The exercise was to take a small mammal and a piece of soft fruit, combine their genes and create a new and cuddly yet delicious lifeform.'

'You, Smeak Junior, what have you got to show us?' Doctor Mordant's left head asked.

'Well,' said young Smeak, placing what looked like a bowl of mangoes on the laboratory bench, 'I crossed a kitten and a mango. I call them Mittens.'

'But they look just like mangoes,' said Doctor Mordant. 'I see no evidence of kitten at all.'

'Try and eat one, sir,' said Smeak.

Doctor Mordant picked up a Mitten and held it to his nose.

'Smells wonderful,' he said. 'Exactly like a mango at the perfect point of ripeness.'

'Take a bite, sir.'

As Doctor Mordant opened his left mouth, there was a violent flash. The Mitten appeared to turn itself inside out and attacked Doctor Mordant's

nose with a flurry of flying claws that sent splashes of blood everywhere. As soon as the doctor dropped the creature, it reverted back into an innocent-looking piece of fruit.

'Just think of the market potential,' said Smeak, as the poor doctor dabbed at his bleeding face. 'Slip one in a bowl of fruit at a party or a business meeting – absolute chaos.'

'Brilliant,' said Doctor Mordant, who had no problem with a bit of pain and blood-letting in the pursuit of science. 'Ten out of ten and a silver star.'

The whole class cheered.

'Who wants to go next?'

Everyone looked at everyone else. Smeak Junior's Mitten had been brilliant and no one wanted to follow it.

'Come on,' said Doctor Mordant. 'Letitia, what about you?'

'Well, I've only got a photo. I had a bit of a problem,' the girl replied.

'Explain.'

'Okay, I couldn't find a mammal and Mum

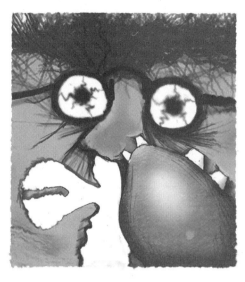

wouldn't let me use the dog after what happened when I crossed the budgie with a crocodile last week.[15] So I had to use a snake and I crossed it with a tomato.'

'Well, that sounds promising,' said Doctor Mordant. 'We weren't going to use reptiles until next term, but never mind. So what went wrong?'

'I called it a Tomython,' said Letitia. 'And it looked brilliant, two metres long and bright red.'

'So where is it?'

'Well, that's the problem,' Letitia explained. 'It looked so brilliant and delicious that every time it caught sight of its own tail, it ate itself.'

---

[15] *You can **imagine** the chaos created by a metre-tall bird, with massively **powerful** jaws full of very sharp teeth, landing on top of people's heads shouting, 'Who's a pretty boy then?'*

The whole class burst out laughing.

'It's not funny,' said Letitia. 'I had seven goes and it did the same thing each time.'

'And then what happened?' said Doctor Mordant.

'I ran out of tomatoes.'

'Winchflat, I'm sure you have something wonderful to show us,' said Doctor Mordant.

Winchflat Flood was not only head boy, but he was the school genius. He was one of those children who seem to be brilliant at everything. But Winchflat was different from most really clever kids who come top all the time, in that he was pretty cool and all the other kids liked him. Except Orkward Warlock,

of course. Of all the Floods, Winchflat was the one Orkward hated most.

'As you know, I've been trying to clone Clarissa, the dodo I managed to hatch out of a three-hundred-and-fifty-year-old egg,' Winchflat began. 'Well, last weekend I cracked it. I put fifty dodos aside to send back to Mauritius, where they came from, and I had a few spares.[16] So I crossed one of them with a cabbage.'

He reached into a big sack and lifted out his creation – the Dabbage. It was even uglier and more ungainly than a dodo. It had two short fat legs and a big lumpy beak, but instead of feathers it had green cabbage leaves. The creature hopped down from Winchflat's desk, waddled across the room and fell over.

'That's useless,' sneered Orkward Warlock.

---

[16] *Merlinmary Flood is trying to train some of Winchflat's spare birds as homing dodos. They're very good at finding their way back but, because they can't fly and are rather fat, they can only find their way home from about two hundred metres away. Merlinmary is now trying to teach dodos to read maps.*

81

Winchflat just smiled.

'And what did you make, Orkward?' Doctor Mordant asked.

'Umm, well …' Orkward began.

'Bring it out here, boy,' said Doctor Mordant.

Orkward put a matchbox on the teacher's desk. Doctor Mordant peered inside.

'A baked bean? You made a baked bean?'

'No,' said Orkward. 'I crossed a baked bean with a flea.'

Before Doctor Mordant could ask him why, the baked bean leapt out of the matchbox and began hopping around the room. The class erupted as everyone tried to catch Orkward's Flean. The Mittens and several other creations popped out of their fruity forms and scrambled out of the way, but some were trampled underfoot. The Parrotato flew out of the window through the narrow bars and landed on the grass as a pile of chips with feathers, and the Bunion[17] crawled up Doctor Mordant's trouser leg.

In the midst of the chaos the Dabbage plodded quietly around the room eating all the squashed experiments. It all ended when the great creature opened its beak and the Flean hopped right down its throat. The Dabbage let out a dreadful green belch, which made everyone's eyes water. It then jumped on top of the smallest child in the room, Howard Tiny, and tried to hatch him out.

---

[17] *A cross between a bat and an onion.*

'Calm down, class,' said Doctor Mordant, turning towards the blackboard. 'Let's move on. This week's homework is to take a herring and an accountant and swap their brains over.'

'Why?' said Orkward.

'Good question, er, er …'

'Orkward Warlock,' said Orkward.

'Yes, Orlock Warkward,' said Doctor Mordant. 'The point of the experiment is to release our modified fish and accountants back into the wild and see if anyone can tell the difference.'[18]

'And of course,' he continued, 'I trust you are all working on your creatures for sports day. Last year we produced the Centithlete, a creature with one hundred legs that could outrun the fastest sprinter. Let's see if we can do better this year.'

'I have one,' said Orkward.

'Really, um, er, Orkflit. Do tell.'

---

[18] *It should be noted that this experiment had been done three hundred years earlier by Doctor Mordant's predecessor and that most of the accountants currently alive do actually have fish brains.*

'A Tyrunningosaurus,' said Orkward. 'Not only will it run faster than everyone else, but it will eat them all as well.'

'You haven't actually made one, have you?' asked Doctor Mordant nervously.

'No, sir. It's just an idea.'

'Well, I think maybe it's a bit too violent,' said Doctor Mordant.

'I have another one, sir,' said Orkward. 'You take all the sand out of the short jump pit and fill it with piranhas.'

'Yes, er, thank you, Orwhat.'

Doctor Mordant and Winchflat carried the Dabbage down to the front office and duplicated it on the Special 3D Photocopier that Winchflat had recently invented to clone his pet dodo Clarissa, before releasing the two of them on the edge of the dark forest. There, they evolved into the Giant Green Patagonian Condor that we all know and fear today. Because Winchflat had the only surviving creature in Genetic Engineering that week, he got ten out of ten and a gold star.

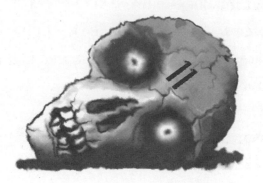

Back in his room, Orkward thought about He Who Must Not Be Talked About while he waited for The Toad to be treated in sick bay. Maybe his daydreams were true. Maybe He Who Must Not Be Talked About was the great wizard on the white dragon – his father.

'You are, like, so pathetic,' said The Mirror, which could read Orkward's mind.

'I'll smash you into a million pieces, you recycled milk bottle,' Orkward snarled between gritted teeth.

'No you won't,' said The Mirror.

'Give me one good reason why not,' said Orkward.

'One? I can give you three.'

'What?'

'Three, you little loser,' said The Mirror. 'One: I am seriously powerful and magic and, like, totally unbreakable. Two: you are a pathetic coward and wouldn't dare.'

'Why are you always so awful to me?' asked Orkward.

'Well, there are three reasons. One: you totally deserve it. Two: it's my job. And –'

'What's the third reason?'

'If you hadn't interrupted me, I was just about to say,' said The Mirror. 'Three: because I enjoy it.'

'No, no, no. What's the third reason why I won't smash you into a million pieces?'

'Ahh, that one. Well, the third reason is that I know who He Who Must Not Be Talked About is.'

'Who? Who? Tell me. Tell me!' shouted Orkward.

'Maybe I will and maybe I, like, won't,' said The Mirror.

'Tell me NOW or I'll smash you into a million pieces!' screamed Orkward.

'Oh man, we have totally been through that already. You can't smash me into pieces, remember?'

'Tell me,' said Orkward and, gritting his teeth and crossing his fingers behind his back so it wouldn't count, he added, 'please.'

'Well, well,' said The Mirror. 'Nice. I didn't know you could do nice, even if you have got your fingers crossed behind your back and don't really mean it. Still, it's a start.'

'Are you going to tell me?'

'Probably, but you have to do something for me.'

'Okay,' said Orkward. 'What?'

'Clean me and hang me back up on the wall so I can see out of the window again.'

'All right.'

'You have to do it before I tell you, because I think you're going to be, like, totally disappointed,' said The Mirror.

Orkward dragged The Mirror out from under the bed, hung it back on the wall and began to dust it with a square of frayed black velvet – the security blanket he had wrapped round his thumb when he went to sleep for as long as he could remember.

'You've missed a bit,' The Mirror said seventeen times before finally adding, 'Cool, now I can see right over the rooftops and into the totally dark forest.'

89

'Okay, who is He Who Must Not Be Talked About?'

'The chairman of the school governors, Councillor P.J. Plausible,' said The Mirror.

'What a ridiculously implausible name,' said Orkward. 'So why is he called He Who Must Not Be Talked About?'

'I don't know. No one will talk about it. I do know he took the clouds away for an afternoon as a punishment because he said the school was going soft.'

'Now I'm really depressed,' said Orkward. 'I'll have to go and hurt something.'

'I know something else,' said The Mirror, 'but it will cost you more than you can afford.'

'What?'

'He Who Must Not Be Talked About is not your father, but I know who is.'

'I don't believe you,' said Orkward.

'Fair enough,' said The Mirror, staring out of the window at the Giant Green Patagonian Condors circling over the forest.

'You don't really know, do you?'

'Oh yes, I, like, totally do,' said The Mirror.

'Tell me … please.'

'Absolutely, no problem,' said The Mirror. 'Just pay my price and I'll tell you straight away.'

'What's your price?' Orkward asked with a dreadful sense of foreboding.

'It's no big deal. You just have to, like, get me something from Narled's treasure trove.'

'But no one knows where it is,' said Orkward.

'Someone does.'

'Who?'

'Narled.'

'Yes, but, I mean, oh God,' said Orkward, slumping down in his chair and putting his head in his hands in total despair. He desperately wanted to know who his father was, but hundreds of people had tried to find Narled's treasure trove, and no one had succeeded. There were rumours, of course, and two students had actually disappeared while searching for it. Another had tried to follow Narled into the dark forest and come back as a sad electronics salesman forever lost in a never-ending quest for a larger plasma television than anyone else had ever seen. Someone had even come back Belgian.

'But what do you want it for?' he added. 'You're a mirror.'

'How many other talking mirrors have you, like, met?' The Mirror asked.

'Well, erm, none actually.'

'Exactly. I might totally look like a mirror. I might even, like, totally be a mirror, but I used to be a man.'

'Really?'

'Yeah man, really,' said The Mirror. 'I used to be this really cool handsome rich dude.'

'So what happened?' said Orkward.

'Oh, you know, the usual story. Some wizard dude fancied my girlfriend but she was, like, totally in love with me and wouldn't have anything to do with him. So he turned me into a mirror. Actually he turned me into a lobster but agreed to change me into a mirror if my girlfriend said she would marry him.'

'Why a mirror?'

'Well, the wizard dude threatened to cook me in a rather nice parsley sauce and my girlfriend said she would be his if he would spare me, and the wizard dude said okay, he would change me into a mirror so he could admire his reflection in me every day.'

'So how did you end up here?'

'Long story, way too complicated,' said The

Mirror. 'But there was a lot of blood and tons of celery involved. I don't want to talk about it, man.'

'I still don't see how Narled's treasure will help you,' said Orkward.

'The wizard dude thought my girlfriend would eventually fall in love with him, but when she didn't he turned her into a china doll. One day he put her down on the grass for a moment and the next moment, Narled had picked her up and taken her away. And, like, the thing is, if we are put together again, we will totally change back into our real selves.'

'Oh, wonderful,' sneered Orkward. 'The love story of the century – a nasty mirror and a china dolly. Hooray.'

'Fair enough,' said The Mirror.

'No, no, I'm sorry,' Orkward lied. 'I'll try.'

'This is, like, such a totally pointless exercise,' said The Mirror. 'You couldn't find your way out of a paper bag, never mind track down Narled's legendary treasure trove.'

'Yes I can,' said Orkward. 'I'll come up with a plan.'

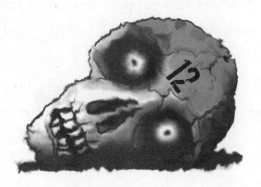

The Toad lay face-down on a bed in sick bay while Matron rubbed her legendary linseed oil and beeswax into his burnt back. Although Matron looked remarkably like a small concrete shed, she had a heart of gold and the children at Quicklime's adored her. She had two assistants, Nurse Romeo and Nurse Juliet, who were two large black crows that could sew skin together with stitches so delicate they were impossible for the human eye to see. Because of the physical, hands-on nature of a lot of the classes and some of the unusual sports at Quicklime's, this was something they did every day. They were also expert at taking people's temperatures with the thermometer in places that could make your eyes water.

'How did this happen, dear?' Matron asked. She had a soft spot for The Toad, having patched him up so often.

'I'd rather not say, Matron,' said The Toad. As the wonderful Enchanted Wax soaked into his skin, the pain slowly faded until the poor toad felt himself floating away in a cloud of turpentine.

'Were you playing with matches again?'

'No, Matron.'

'You weren't up to your old firework-making tricks again, were you?'

'No, Matron. I have toad's feet, remember?'

said The Toad, adding wistfully, 'I can't even light matches any more.'

'Someone did this to you, didn't they?' asked Matron gently.

The Toad didn't answer.

'It was that vile Orkward Warlock, wasn't it?' said Matron. 'It's all right, you don't have to say. It's obvious. You just lie there and rest while I go and get the nasty little devil.'

As soon as Matron had left, The Toad climbed down off the bed, grabbed the tin of wax and made for the door.

'Where do you think you're going, sunshine?' said Nurse Romeo.

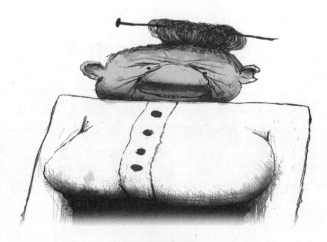

'I'm better now,' said The Toad. 'I should get back to class.'

'And what do you think you're doing with Matron's Enchanted Wax?' said Nurse Juliet.

'Umm, oh, I must have picked it up by mistake,' said The Toad, reaching for the door handle behind his back.

'Put it down.'

'I'll just, erm, er, take it to Matron,' said The Toad. 'She might need it.' And he ran out the door.

As the two nurses flew after him, he managed to hide behind a statue and give them the slip. When he was sure there was no one about he made his way to the secret place up in the thirteenth clock tower,[19] where Orkward was waiting for him.

'Brilliant,' said Orkward. 'You're almost useful. Now get lost.'

---

[19] *The school has thirteen clock towers because, unlike the rest of the world, Quicklime's runs on a twenty-six-hour day. Each tower rings on its own hour with a different note so that wherever you are in the valley you always know what the time is to within fifty-eight minutes (each hour has fifty-nine minutes).*

'Can I come with you?' said The Toad. 'I could carry the polish.'

'I suppose,' Orkward agreed. If they got caught at least he could blame it all on The Toad.

It took a while to slip out of the school without being seen, but finally they reached the path in the dark forest where Orkward had spoken to Narled the day before.

'Right, we sit here and wait,' said Orkward.

'Do you really think he'll come?'

'Yes,' Orkward replied with great confidence. He didn't actually think Narled *was* going to come, but sure enough a few minutes later there was a rustling in the bushes and there he was.

He was not alone.

There was another suitcase creature with him, slightly smaller than Narled, and around their feet were six little handbags.

Orkward and The Toad were speechless.

Narled was not, as everyone assumed, the result of an experiment gone wrong, but a real animal. *Sacculus Pluscruris Patagonius* was a very rare

100

species of creature that only survived in the safety of Quicklime's remote valley. Once, similar species had lived on every major continent but they had been hunted to extinction everywhere except for this one place. Their skins had been made into suitcases and holdalls, and even their babies had been made into little bags and purses. Nowadays suitcases are usually made of nylon and plastic, but in the past, the more endangered the animal, the more desirable was the luggage.

'I've ... I've, er, got the polish,' Orkward mumbled as the tiny handbags ran between his legs.

The Toad sat down and reached out to stroke them. One of them climbed onto his lap and nuzzled into him. It smelled of warm leather and brought a lump into The Toad's throat that stirred up a feeling he'd spent the last few years trying to forget. When he had blown up the toilets and been turned into a toad as a punishment, his parents had been unable to accept it. His father had rejected him instantly and his mother, although she had tried really hard to keep loving him, had found it impossible to pick him up and cuddle him ever again. Since then, he had spent every school holiday in a pond at the bottom of his

parents' garden with a lot of toads who were real toads and really, really stupid.

Now this little handbag's affection brought it all back and The Toad felt tears welling up in his eyes. He tried to hide them. He knew how Orkward would sneer at him and, as horrible as Orkward was, he was the closest thing The Toad had to a friend. But two more of the tiny handbags climbed into his lap and The Toad couldn't stop himself.

He wept uncontrollably.

The first handbag opened itself, took out a tissue and handed it to The Toad. This kindness only made

him cry more. Narled's wife came over and patted him on the arm. She undid her zip, took out pen and paper and wrote: 'We feel your pain. We are here for you.'

What had made the near extinction of their species even sadder was that *Sacculus Pluscruris Patagonius* had finely tuned emotions, much finer than ours, that could not only pick up other creatures' feelings, but get inside their heads and discover the reasons for those feelings and then respond in a deep and meaningful way.

Meanwhile, Orkward was so obsessed with his plan that he noticed none of this. He was too busy polishing Narled and pretending to be his friend. Of course, being super-sensitive, Narled didn't believe a word of what Orkward was saying, but hey, he was getting the best polishing he'd had in a hundred years.

The delirious smell of turpentine seeped through the little gaps in his zip and into his brain, where it brought back long-buried memories of centuries past when every suitcase family had had a faithful servant who had polished them every day. Even in those days Matron's Enchanted Wax had been legendary, the finest polish of all, which only the most noble suitcases were allowed to use. Thoughts of the past and its former glories filled his heart with sadness. How had it come to this, a life of picking up after those who had once been their servants?

'Right,' said Orkward. 'It's agreed. I will bring you a small package and you will take it to the Floods when they are in the middle of the stadium next week on sports day.'

Narled wrinkled up, and Orkward took this to mean that Narled would do what he wanted, but Narled was just wrinkling his skin to make sure the polish got right down into his creases.

'And to show how much I really, really like you,' said Orkward, who had just thought of another plan, 'I'll come back tomorrow and polish you again.'

Mrs Narled, or Narlene as she was known to the rest of the cloakroom,[20] handed The Toad another piece of paper: 'Don't be a stranger.'

And the family trundled off into the dark forest.

'I expect you're wondering why I said I'd come and polish that suitcase again,' said Orkward, completely unaware of The Toad's unhappiness. 'Well, I have an absolutely brilliant plan.'

The Toad said nothing. All he could think of was going back and being with the baby handbags.

---

[20] *Just as you get a flock of sheep and a pride of lions and a lump of PE teachers, so you get a cloakroom of* Sacculus Pluscruris Patagonius.

'Listen,' Orkward raved on. 'I'm a genius – more of a genius than that idiot Winchflat Flood! Next time I polish Narled, I'm going to fix a tracking device to his straps, then the idiot will lead us straight to his treasure.'

'Oh,' said The Toad as they walked back to the road.

'Wait,' said Orkward. He took a jar out of his pocket, scooped a big lump of polish out of Matron's tin and put it in the jar.

'You better take the Enchanted Wax back,' he said. 'I'm going to hide this here in the bushes for next time.'

'I think I'll just creep up and leave it outside Matron's door,' said The Toad. 'She's a bit formidable when she's angry.'

Lesson: Economics and Other Forms of Burglary

Teacher: Aubergine Wealth

The two strongest boys in the class stood behind Aubergine Wealth, who was stuck in the doorway, and pushed. This was always happening, not because he was too fat, but because he had so much money, his wallet wouldn't fit through the door.

'Thank you, boys, and a gold star to each of you for stealing my gold watch and signet ring without my realising it,' he said. 'Today, we will continue working on our plan to remove all the gold from Fort Knox, but first I'd like Morbid and Silent to give us their report on how they got on "borrowing" the Crown Jewels from the Tower of London.'

Morbid and Silent went to the front of the class. They were each wearing a priceless crown. Morbid was carrying the royal sceptre and Silent the golden ball.

'Well, as you can see,' announced Morbid, 'we achieved our goal.'

The rest of the class, except Orkward Warlock, cheered. The only treasure Orkward had ever managed to steal was a jar of marmalade from the school kitchen. Although he was useless at theft and international money laundering, and consistently failed Aubergine Wealth's class, this was not really Orkward's fault. When the boy had been sent to the school at the age of three days, his parents had paid Quicklime's headmaster, Professor Throat, NB, PDF, PS, to cast a spell that made it impossible for Orkward to leave the valley. The last thing they wanted was their beloved son turning up unexpectedly.[21]

'We also got this,' said Morbid, dragging a chair out from behind a cupboard. 'King Edward's coronation chair.'

Silent grunted and proudly held up the chair, which had a small pink cauliflower sitting on it.

'Oh yes,' Morbid added. 'We also got a bonus –

---

[21] *Orkward's parents tried not to think about the day their son would finally leave school and return home with his nasty little head full of revenge. 'We'll blow that bridge up when he comes to it,' said his mother.*

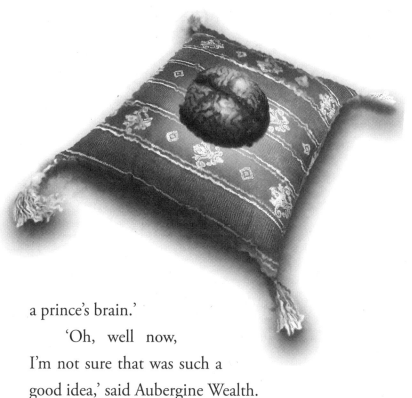

a prince's brain.'

'Oh, well now, I'm not sure that was such a good idea,' said Aubergine Wealth.

'Well, sir, we thought that too. So we put it back, but no one could tell the difference, so we thought, what the hell, and kept it.'

'No, no,' said Aubergine. 'That's not what I meant. The reason I said it wasn't such a good idea is that it's not really worth anything, is it?'

'Actually, sir,' said Morbid, 'we've had seven

bids for it on eBay. It's up to seven hundred dollars so far.'

Silent was so excited that he nearly spoke. Not that anyone could tell, though later on when they got home Silent handed his twin a piece of paper, which said: 'I got so excited today I nearly spoke.'

'Ah! Now that, boys and girls, is what this class is all about – enterprise and the unbridled joy of making lots of money,' said Aubergine Wealth. 'Well done the Flood twins, ten out of ten and two gold stars.'

Orkward was livid. It seems that whatever the lesson was, the wretched Floods always got top marks and a gold star. He could feel the veins in his head beginning to throb and that meant only one thing. As soon as he possibly could, he would have to kick someone smaller than he was.

All The Toad could think of was going back to Narled and his family. Matron's polish could wait. While Orkward was busy hiding his jar and marking the spot with some twigs so he could find it again, The Toad went round a bend in the path and hid behind a tree. A few minutes later Orkward went by and The Toad walked back into the forest.

When he reached the place where he'd first met the family, it was deserted, but the branches that had parted to let Narled's family through were still open so he followed the path into the darkness. Instead of closing him out like it had with Orkward, the forest opened its arms to him. The branches moved aside, welcomed him in, then closed gently behind him.

The ground was covered with the little footprints and tiny wheel tracks of Narled's family. Here and there other paths crossed the main one, and they too were covered with the same marks, but The Toad kept walking straight ahead.

He had never been into the dark forest before and didn't know anyone who had, student or teacher. Even Orkward Warlock, who spent the whole of every holiday at Quicklime's, had never been any further than the closed branches. The entire forest was out of bounds, and even to wizards and witches it was an ominous and terrifying place, a kind of impenetrable nightmare that surrounded the entire school. There were those who thought the dark forest was not a forest at all but some huge living creature.

The Toad was the sort of animal who always thought the best of everyone. If someone hit him over the head, he would admire the stick they had hit him with. It simply didn't occur to him that things could be deliberately bad or unfair. When he'd been turned into a toad – which was a very, very extreme punishment for accidentally blowing up a few toilets,

especially considering that the only injury caused was a nasty burn on Orkward's bottom, which everyone agreed the boy deserved – even then he hadn't complained.

'I suppose I deserve it,' he had said, flicking a fly off the ceiling with his tongue. 'You know, I'd never realised just how delicious flies were,' he added, looking on the bright side.

Now as he walked deeper and deeper into the gloom, it simply didn't occur to him to be scared. After all, why would anyone want to harm him? He was just a little toad.

'Hello?' he called out from time to time, but there was no answer.

Dinner time came and went. The dark forest grew darker and The Toad began to falter. His little legs had been aching for a while but he had been so intent on his mission he hadn't noticed. He turned a corner, tripped over a tree root and fell flat on his face.

'Oh well,' he said to himself. 'Seeing as how I'm already lying down, I might as well have a little rest.'

He curled up in some wet leaves. In seconds he was fast asleep.

Lesson: Elocution[22] and Howling
Teacher: Mademoiselle Fifi la Venus

The noise was deafening. The entire class was howling, screaming and wailing at the top of their voices, not in harmony like a choir, but each student practising his or her own specialty.

This was the only subject that Orkward Warlock was any good at. He could scream with such a piercing whine that he could make goldfish explode, and often did. He hoped today's class would be focusing on screaming.

Mademoiselle Fifi la Venus held up her wings and waited for the class to quieten down. They

[22] *Talking proper.*

didn't, so she fluttered up to the ceiling and opened her mouth. Instantly, before she could utter a sound, everyone stopped in mid-scream. They all knew only too well what could happen when the Mademoiselle shouted. Almost every child in the class had had at least one eardrum transplant in Matron's sick bay.

'Right,' said Mademoiselle Fifi la Venus, 'now we have loosened up our voices, we will begin today's lesson. Orkward, get a cloth and wipe the goldfish off the back of Howard's head.'

Orkward didn't so much wipe Howard's head as push it down inside his shirt and jacket. Howard started counting to himself, which he always did when it got dark suddenly.

'Today, children, we are going to practise throwing our voices,' the Mademoiselle continued. 'We've all learned how to throw our voices around

the valley without losing them. Except you, Howard. How is your new voice, by the way?'

'It's a bit odd, miss, fourteen, fifteen, sixteen,' squeaked Howard. 'Every time I speak, I think it's someone else talking. What? Who said that?'

'Well, until you find your own voice again, you'll just have to make do with that one.'

'Yes, miss. What, twenty-seven, twenty-eight?'

'Be quiet, Howard,' said the Mademoiselle.

'I didn't say anything, miss. Did I? What, forty-three?' Howard squeaked.

'Now, class, we are going to learn to throw our voices further away.'

'Are we going to practise on goldfish?' Orkward asked.

'Shush please, Orkwood. By the end of term I want every one of you to be able to throw your voice back to your own home. I want you to be able to say something to your parents from the other side of the world.'

Orkward Warlock felt a lump coming into his throat. Not only had he been sent away from his own

home at the age of three days, he didn't even know where that home was. He had a terrible feeling that he was going to cry and had to bite his lip so hard it bled. The absolutely, totally, completely last thing he ever wanted was for any of the other children or teachers to see him cry. Pretty well everyone knew he cried quite often and they thought they should feel sorry for him, but because he was so horrible, they absolutely, totally, completely wouldn't. Except The Toad, who thought Orkward was wonderful, even if he did keep exploding the goldfish The Toad was about to eat for lunch.

'We are going to aim to all throw our voices at the same place. First, we will practise with harmonised humming. When we've mastered that, we'll go on to throwing actual words. Follow me,' she said, pointing to a map of Patagonia and beyond. 'We will aim south and all focus on this point here in Antarctica.'

The twenty-seven children and their teacher began to hum in perfect synchronisation. Softly and low at first, then gradually rising in volume and

pitch until they sounded like a single high-pitched ear-splitting scream. The windows began to vibrate and then shattered, not into hundreds of pieces like a normal high note would do, but into a fine dust that blew away in the wind.

A line of trees in the dark forest shivered, shedding leaves as the voice, now too high for normal ears to hear, climbed up the side of the valley and over the mountains towards Tierra del Fuego. The sound tore a furrow across the sea as it flew towards the South Pole and finally reached the exact point that Mademoiselle Fifi la Venus was pointing at on the map.

The ground shook and cracked as a massive shelf of ice broke free and began to float north.

'Merlinmary, you threw your voice the furthest last week, so would you like to take over?' the Mademoiselle asked.

Merlinmary went to the front of the class and put her finger on the map, which, because of all the electricity she generated, began to smoulder around the edges. She moved her finger north and, as she did

so, the greatest iceberg in history moved north too and began to rotate.

Faster and faster it spun, creating a wider and wider circle of waves. By the time it reached the

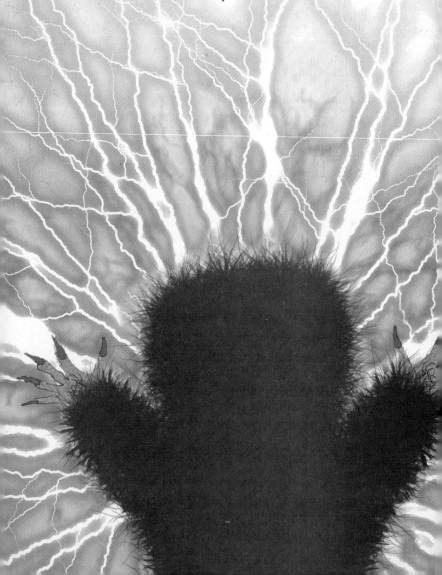

Equator, the iceberg was spinning so fast that it rose up in the air. Without the sea to hold it back, it flew with incredible speed towards Africa. The class's humming followed it, gradually turning into screaming that shook the wallpaper off the classroom walls. When the flying iceberg reached the middle of the Sahara desert, Merlinmary held up her arms and everyone stopped screaming.

Bolts of lightning leapt from Merlinmary's fingertips and flew around the room. They shot up the chimney, taking the blazing log fire with them, and up into the sky. Clouds, heavy with impending rain, exploded into steam as the lightning raced across the ocean towards the iceberg. Merlinmary clicked her fingers, shorting out the circuit, and the iceberg exploded.

It shattered into a million pieces that came crashing down into the desert, narrowly missing some very surprised camels.

The only people to see it were a team of geologists who were about to ruin the beautiful desert by drilling for oil. When they tried to tell the world about an iceberg the size of fifty football fields falling out of the sky, they were recalled to Texas and locked up in a very secure hospital, though no one ever came up with an explanation of why fifteen penguins and a seal were found wandering about in the middle of a desert.

'Merlinmary Flood, that was fantastic,' said Mademoiselle Fifi la Venus. 'Ten out of ten and a gold star.'

'Ten out of ten and a gold star, nah, nah, nah,' Orkward Warlock muttered under his breath and kicked the smallest girl in the class on the shins.

'Gold stars, gold stars,' he cursed to himself as he went back to his room to kick The Toad. 'You'll see a million gold stars on sports day!'

'Where on Earth am I going to get a tracking device?' Orkward said to no one in particular.

'Well, you're not clever enough to, like, build one,' said The Mirror.

'Shut up, shut up,' said Orkward.

'The only person who could build one,' The Mirror continued, 'is Winchflat Flood, and I happen to know that he's actually made one before to keep track of his sister Betty when she was a baby.'

'Shut up, shut up, shut up!'

'I'm sure he'd lend it to you,' sneered The Mirror, 'seeing as how you like him so much.'

'Hippie lavatory brain,' said Orkward and wrote a rude word on The Mirror with his greasy finger.

The door flew open and Matron marched in, followed by Romeo and Juliet.

'There you are, you evil little boy,' she said. 'I want to see you about burning The Toad, but first of all I want you to tell me where he is. He ran away with my Enchanted Wax and I suspect you had something to do with it.'

'I don't know what you're talking about,' Orkward lied.

'We'll see about that,' said Matron, grabbing

Orkward by the ear and dragging him out the door. 'You need to visit the sick bay, my boy,' she added.

'But I'm not sick,' Orkward protested.

'I know that,' said Matron, 'but you're going to be.'

As well as all the ordinary medicines like aspirins and sticking plasters, Matron had a whole range of special wizard and witch remedies. As she dragged Orkward along, the boy tried to put a spell on her. He muttered the ancient French spell that turns people into a pig's bladder, and the deadly Welsh spell that makes you wear a hat with a torch on it and sing dreadful songs for weeks on end, but Matron was immune to everything. He even tried the spell that no one realises you're doing because it sounds as if you're sneezing – the famous spell that turns you inside out. But Matron had seen every spell that had ever been invented, and had inoculated herself against all of them. She had even come up with some pretty wild spells of her own.

'You might as well stop all that,' she said. 'Far better wizards than you have tried. Okay, Nurse

Romeo, I think we'll give him a spoonful of cough medicine first.'

'But I haven't got a cough,' said Orkward.

'No, of course you haven't. That's why we're giving you cough medicine, to make you cough up the truth.'

Nurse Juliet poked her beak in Orkward's right ear while Nurse Romeo pecked the top of his head on the other side.

'AHHHHOOOWWWWWWWW,' Orkward cried and, as he did so, Matron tipped a glass of cough mixture into his open mouth.

'We'll just give that a minute to start working,' she said. 'Though, come to think of it, nasty little liars like you sometimes need a second dose.'

So the nurses attacked him again and Matron gave him another lot. It was disgusting – not just the awful taste, which was like a cross between strawberries and cow manure, but the terrifying feeling it sent through Orkward's brain. It was as if every closed door inside his head was suddenly thrown wide open and he knew that no matter how hard he tried to

fight it, he would tell the truth to whatever question he was asked.

'Where is The Toad?' said Matron.

'I don't know,' said Orkward. 'The last time I saw him, he was on his way here to bring back your wax.'

'Well, he never arrived.'

'It's the truth,' Orkward whimpered. 'Honest.'

'I can see that,' said Matron. 'Well, let's start from the last time you saw him.'

Orkward didn't want to tell her about going into the forest to polish Narled, but every time he stopped telling the truth, he began to cough, not just a bit of cough like you get with a cold, but a deep down cough that brought up his breakfast and bits of last night's dinner.

'We were in the forest …' he began.

But the last thing he wanted was for anyone to know he had been to see Narled. So gritting his teeth, he tried to lie.

Cough, bacon, cough, carrots, cough …

'You went into the forest?' said Matron. 'You know that's not allowed, don't you?'

'We were only a tiny bit in,' said Orkward. 'No more than a hundred metres.'

'And that's where you saw The Toad for the last time?'

'Yes. He set off back here, just before me.'

'You stayed behind to bury a jar with some of my stolen wax in it, didn't you?'

'No, I …'

Cough, banana, cough, carrot, splutter …

'I, er, didn't …'

Cough, porridge, cough, shoelace,[23] and then Orkward collapsed on the floor.

'Yes,' he whispered.

'Right,' said Matron. 'That's enough for now. Get into bed and rest while the cough mixture wears off. We'll talk about punishment for you burning him later. And don't go bothering Winchflat in the other bed. He's resting his genius brain. He was splitting

---

[23] *Shoelace???*

the atom all morning and then invented an anti-gravity engine after lunch, and he's totally exhausted. I don't want to hear a sound from you. You can stay here while we go and find The Toad.'

Matron locked her patients in and went to see Professor Throat. The thought of anyone, never mind an innocent like The Toad, being out in the dark forest all night, was very worrying. The two nurses flew around the school asking everyone if they had seen the poor creature.

No one had.

'And I'll tell you something very unusual,' Prebender Glorious told them with a sigh, 'I haven't seen Narled either. It's probably a coincidence, but he *always* checks the quadrangle at the end of lessons without fail. Seventy-five years I've been here, and every single night I've looked out of my window and seen him making a final check round the place before dark.'

After school, Professor Throat gathered everyone in the Grate Hall. The fire that burned in the Great Grate had been alight since Quicklime's had been built seven hundred and fifty years ago. Doorlock the handyman was the fifteenth generation of his family to care for the fire, and not once in all that time had the fire ever died. Even in summer when the temperature in the remote Patagonian valley soared up as high as five degrees, the fire was kept alight. Generations of children and teachers had been warmed by its magical flames and hypnotised by the dancing elves that lived in its fiery heart.

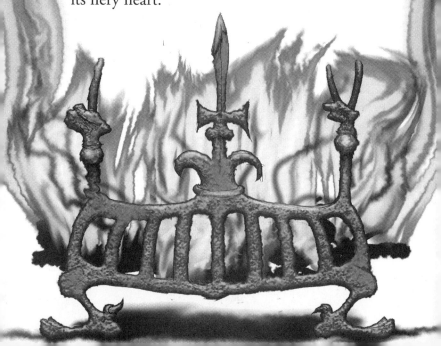

Among the staff and students, there were dozens of witches and wizards who could send their thoughts out into the world and find things.

This was how the school had become so immensely wealthy – so wealthy that it didn't have a bank account in Switzerland, it actually owned Switzerland, though they kept very quiet about it. Quicklime's economics teacher, Aubergine Wealth, had sent his thoughts out into bank vaults to look over people's shoulders when they were putting in the secret numbers to open combination locks. Then, when everyone was asleep, he sent his body over to join his thoughts and robbed them all blind.

'I only do it for a great cause,' he confided in Professor Throat. 'I am robbing the rich to help the even richer ... us.'

There was only one place in the whole world where no one could send their thoughts, and that was into the dark forest.

Everyone sat very still and concentrated. The fire in the grate burned down to ash, almost dying before Doorlock came in with armfuls of fresh logs.

The school buses sat impatiently in the quadrangle and around the world parents began to wonder what was keeping their children.[24] Night fell in an enveloping silence while everyone searched the world high and low for The Toad. At midnight the children were all sent home and the staff made one final search.

'He has to be in the dark forest,' said Professor Throat.

He began to feel rather guilty. Maybe turning the boy into a toad had been too harsh a punishment. Maybe it had driven him over the edge. Though one thing didn't quite add up.

'What I don't understand,' he said, 'is that *if* he is in the dark forest, how did he get there? We all know it locks its branches against anyone who tries to enter.'

'Not everyone,' said Matron. 'Orkward Warlock

---

[24] *Quicklime's parents never worry when their children don't come home, for two reasons. One, the kids are witches and wizards so they can look after themselves; and two, Quicklime's students often stay behind at school for strange midnight ceremonies and rituals.*

told me that Narled went into the forest. He said it opened its branches for him and then closed them again before they could follow him.'

'You can't believe anything that boy says,' said Prebender Glorious.

'You can when he's had a dose of my cough mixture.'

'Ahh,' said Prebender Glorious, remembering his own childhood at the school and Matron's formidable pharmacy. 'So maybe Narled has taken The Toad.'

'I've never heard of him collecting children before,' said Professor Throat. 'It's usually iPods and socks and bits of paper.'

'And quite a lot of unfinished homework,' Doctor Mordant laughed. 'We've all heard that excuse, haven't we?'

'Yes, yes,' said Professor Throat, 'but never children.'

'But he isn't a child, is he?' said Matron. 'He's a toad.'

'I know. I know,' said the Professor. 'But I don't

think Narled has ever taken any sort of living creature before.'

They talked into the early hours and decided that at first light they would cover the valley from top to bottom to see if they could find The Toad or any way of getting into the dark forest.

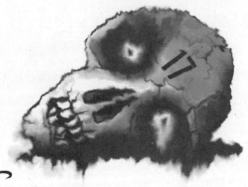

When he looked back later, The Toad was never sure which bits of that night had been real and which bits had been a dream. It had been too wonderful to be real, but then it had been too wonderful to be a dream too. The Toad's dreams usually involved hopping across a very, very wide road very, very slowly while a huge truck with fifty massive black tyres hurtled towards him going very, very fast.

The last thing he remembered that he knew was real was tripping over a tree root.

Lots of little arms lifted the sleeping toad gently off the damp leaves and carried him deeper into the forest. He remembered voices like babies talking, voices that seemed to be inside his head, twittering

baby talk that didn't make words, just joyful twittering noises. And he remembered feeling happier than he had ever felt before.

Then he was in a cave on a bed of soft grass and the six baby handbags were curled up around him and their mother was singing softly to send them all to sleep. And the song was there inside The Toad's head, stroking his brain and washing away his sadness. And when the handbags were all asleep with their tiny thumbs stuck in their zips, Narlene beckoned The Toad away to the far side of the cave, where there was food and drink.

'You have a good heart,' she said to The Toad, though the words seemed to appear inside his head.

'Can you all speak?' he asked. 'Even Narled?'

'Only creatures with kind hearts can hear us,' said Narlene. 'That evil scheming boy you were with will never hear us.'

The Toad began to pour his heart out to her. He wanted to tell her what Orkward was up to. He wanted to tell her how his parents had rejected him and how big the lonely thing inside him felt, but he hardly said more than a few words before he fell asleep.

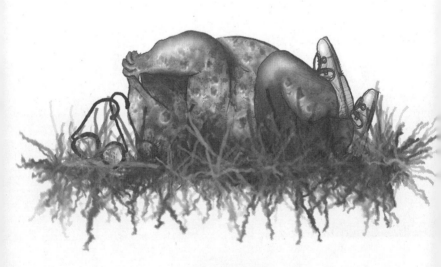

When Orkward woke up it was dark. He couldn't believe his luck. Here he was with Winchflat Flood, the one person he needed more than any other. The trouble was, Winchflat knew he hated him and he knew that Winchflat knew he knew. If Orkward was to persuade the boy to give him the tracking device, he would have to come up with a damn good plan.

Winchflat was still sleeping.

Orkward began to cry. Winchflat stirred but did not wake up. Orkward cried a bit louder.

'Who's that?' said Winchflat in the darkness.

'Oh, it's nobody,' sobbed Orkward.

I recognise that voice, thought Winchflat. *It's that vile Orkward Warlock.*

'Is that you, Orkward?' Winchflat asked, and, pretending he didn't know otherwise, he added, 'No, it can't be. Orkward Warlock would never cry.'

'Well, of course, the old Orkward Warlock never ever cried,' said Orkward, 'but things have changed.'

Naturally Winchflat did not believe a word of this. No one would, except maybe the poor innocent Toad, but he decided to pretend he did, to see what the vile boy was up to. He was just glad it was pitch dark so Orkward couldn't see him grinning.

'Really?' said Winchflat.

'Yes,' Orkward sobbed. 'It's my dear little sister Primrose. She keeps wandering away and I'm frightened that something awful in the dark forest might kill her.'

'Oh dear, that's terrible.'

'What I need is some sort of tracking device, so I can always tell where she is,' said Orkward.

'Well,' said Winchflat, 'by an amazing coincidence, I've got one. I built it when my sister was a toddler. She kept wandering off too.'

'Really?'

'Oh, yes. You wouldn't believe how far she'd go sometimes,' said Winchflat. 'Once we found her right up the top of the Eiffel Tower. Another time she was three hundred feet under the sea in the ladies toilets in the lost city of Atlantis. You know, I've always thought it was very strange that Atlantis was a lost city. I mean, how could anyone lose a whole city, and what on Earth were they doing taking it to the bottom of the sea in the first place? Then another time, we'd looked everywhere and she was right at home inside the fridge eating raspberry and rodent yoghurt. And then –'

'Yes, well. How interesting,' said Orkward, gritting his teeth to stop himself from saying something sarcastic. 'So, er, do you still use it?'

'Oh, no. It's sitting on a shelf in my workshop,' said Winchflat. 'Would you like to borrow it?'

YES! said Orkward inside his head. *God, you're dumb. I don't know why anyone would call you a genius.*

'Gosh, could I?' he said out loud.

146

'No problem,' said Winchflat. 'I'll bring it to school on Friday.'

After I've made a few slight modifications, Winchflat thought.

As soon as the sun rose the next morning and the wizard buses had dropped all the students back at school, groups of teachers and children set out to look for The Toad.

Radius Leg, the sports master and therefore the fittest member of staff, took a team of the older boys to the foot of the White Widowmaker, a sheer cliff of ice at the top of the valley. There was no way The

Toad could have ever climbed the Widowmaker, but Radius Leg was one of those short little people who liked to show off how macho he was.

Of course, any of the boys with him could have flown to the top of the cliff in a few seconds. They were wizards, after all. But Radius Leg said there was to be no magic involved. While he struggled up the deadly ice-face with ropes and climbing equipment, the boys sat under a tree and listened to their iPods. They knew that within fifteen minutes, their teacher would come crashing to the ground and they would have to carry him back to Matron to get mended. It happened all the time. There were enough bits of metal holding Radius together to build a small car.

'Why don't we just leave him here this time?' Morbid Flood suggested. 'Every time we carry him back to get fixed up he weighs more and more.'

Silent nodded vigorously.

'We could always sell him to a scrap metal dealer,' said one of the other boys.

Sure enough, seven minutes later Radius Leg came crashing to the ground. He lay there happily groaning in pain for another seven minutes and then fainted. The valley where Quicklime College lay hidden was the highest valley in Patagonia and the White Widowmaker was at the top end of the valley. Its sheer face sealed them off from the outside world. The air was thin and barely a day passed at that altitude without a serious blizzard.

The boys helped their unconscious teacher by relieving him of his extra weight, taking all the money and caramel toffees out of his pocket. Then they took one last look at him just to make sure he wasn't regaining consciousness, and left.

Within a few hours they were back at school warming themselves in the Grate Hall. They'd

informed Professor Throat of the sports teacher's position, but as winter wasn't that far away and Gristleball wouldn't be played again until next Easter, it was decided to leave him there.

'He'll thaw out in good time,' said the Professor. 'He always does, and it'll save the school a bit on food. You did mark his position with a stick, though, didn't you, just in case?'

Up the mountain, Radius Leg, now buried under a fresh fall of snow, began to hibernate. It was not the first time this had happened. Nor would it be the last.

Satanella Flood led a team of small animals down into the drains beneath the school.[25] This was exactly the sort of place you might expect The Toad to go – warm, dark, and dripping with slime. There were a lot of strange creatures down there who were also warm,

---

[25] *Actually, only one of them, Audrey the hamster, was a real animal. The others, like Satanella, had once been children.*

dark and dripping with slime. Most of them were the descendants of Doctor Mordant's failed experiments that had been small enough to flush down the lavatory. These creatures had grouped together, fallen in love and given birth to even stranger creatures. Their leader, Scarcely, a cross between a roller-skate, a goblin and a paperclip, was one of the blessed few with the power of speech. He and Satanella were old friends.

'No, my dear,' said Scarcely. 'Haven't seen the

little chap down here. Not for a long time. Nice little fellow, he is.'

'Well, if you hear anything, send me an email,' said Satanella.

'Can't, I'm afraid,' said Scarcely. 'Little Scrubby has eaten the modem and my niece has eloped with the mouse.'

Back in his room, Winchflat had made his modifications to the tracking device so it now had a tracking device tracking device. While Orkward Warlock would be able to track Narled once he had fitted the first bit to his straps, Winchflat would also be able to track Orkward with a third bit linked to the second bit Orkward would be using to track Narled.[26]

He then began his own search for The Toad.

---

[26] *If this seems rather complicated and leaves you feeling a bit muddled, take five minutes to run your head under a cold tap before reading any more.*

His search was through cyberspace, through the twenty-seven million chatrooms and five hundred million deadly boring blogs that five hundred million deadly boring people posted every day in the mistaken belief that it would make them any more interesting or somehow help them get a life. The Toad was not in any of these places.

It might seem weird to think the poor creature could have got trapped somewhere in the internet but Winchflat knew only too well that it could happen. Two year earlier his best friend at Quicklime's, Eric Ordinaire, had vanished into a chatroom dedicated to very early computers that could add nine and seventeen at the speed of a dead snail going backwards, and Eric had never been seen again.[27]

'I can safely say,' Winchflat later reported to Professor Throat, 'that The Toad is not in the internet.'

'How comforting,' said the Professor. 'It's a

---

[27] *If you look at the back of this book there is a page about the Mobius Strip which explains how this happens. Once you get in, you can never get out again.*

great relief to know we can cross that off our list. He probably isn't in any of the jam jars in the school kitchens, either.'

'Would you like me to go and look, sir, eighty-six, eighty-seven, eighty-eight?' said Howard Tiny.

'I don't think that will be necessary, Howard,' said Professor Throat.

'Well, he could be, sir,' said Howard. 'I mean, you could get a toad inside a jam jar quite easily, ninety-three, ninety-four, ninety-five.'

'You're absolutely right, Howard. Off you go to check. And take your time, just in case he's hiding under a slice of pickled beetroot,' said the Professor, who, like everyone else, preferred it when Howard Tiny was somewhere else.

The Toad was not in any of the jam jars. Other places he was not included the peanut butter jars and the pickled onion jars but, just to make sure, Howard took the top off each jar, stuck his fingers in and poked around in case The Toad was trapped under a large strawberry or an onion. Then, starting on the top shelf, he counted every jar, which made him so

excited he completely forgot why he was there. So he counted all the jar lids, and finally counted all the letters in all the words on all the labels on all the jars.

It was three weeks before anyone saw him again.[28]

Merlinmary Flood decided to see if The Toad was up any of the chimneys. Quicklime College

---

[28] *Apart from the kitchen maid, who came in to get some marmalade.*

had three hundred and sixty-five chimneys and Merlinmary knew a lot of them like the back of her hand.[29] Some of the chimneys didn't lead up to the outside, and although they were above fireplaces they were definitely not meant to have fires in them. These chimneys were actually tunnels that led to other tunnels that turned and twisted and joined together through the thick stone walls of Quicklime College, ending up in secret places that were so secret no one knew about them. Some tunnels were dead ends. Some were deliberate traps[30] and most of them had not been visited for centuries.

Even the teachers did not know these chimney tunnels existed. They had never felt any desire to crawl around inside dark airless places full of soot, but Merlinmary had. She had discovered the tunnels completely by accident when she had climbed up one for a dare.

---

[29] *The back of Merlinmary's hand was very hairy, which none of the chimneys was. Actually, there was one secret tunnel that was extremely hairy, but that's another story.*
[30] *The Mobius Strip again.*

While her friends stood and watched, she had crawled into the fireplace in the fourth year common room, reached up and vanished into the darkness. An hour later when she hadn't returned, her friends had begun to get worried, but they had been too scared to tell anyone in case they got into trouble. Seven hours later, Merlinmary came in through the door just as her friends had decided they better report her missing after all.

'You'll never guess where I've been,' she said.

She went back into the fireplace, but none of her friends was brave enough to follow her.

Merlinmary's tunnel had taken her out of the school, beneath the dark forest – she knew she was beneath the dark forest by the thick roots growing through the tunnel roof, roots that had moved aside to let her pass – and up into the mountains that surrounded the valley. She had been so deep inside the mountains that there was no signal on her mobile and she had been unable to SMS her mother and say she wouldn't be home for dinner.

Finally, there had been a beam of light at the

end of the tunnel and she had come out into a huge cave full of treasure. She had found Narled's legendary treasure store.

Hiding behind a pile of gold coins, she had watched as the suitcase had come into the cave, undone his zip and taken out the odds and ends he had collected that afternoon. Everyone at Quicklime's talked about Narled's storehouse and tried to guess where it was. Merlinmary was the only one to have found it, but instead of telling anyone, something told her it would be better kept secret.

Merlinmary went through all the tunnels and secret places that she had visited before – she knew there were other places still to discover – but The Toad was in none of them.

Matron and the two nurses woke Orkward Warlock up and gave him some more cough medicine.

'Right, you little beast,' said Matron, 'take us to where you last saw The Toad.'

Orkward shook his head but the medicine was starting to take effect and he coughed up some gravy.

'That's better. Now, we know you went into the forest,' said Matron. 'So just take us to the right place.'

'But I'm not supposed to go in there, remember?' said Orkward. 'You said that.'

'It's a bit late for that. The forest was the last

place you saw The Toad. So that is where we are going to start looking,' said Matron.

Orkward wanted to keep the place secret, because that was where he was planning to fix the tracking device to Narled, but Matron's cough mixture had broken stronger and braver boys than Orkward and five minutes later, still dripping gravy from his nose, he was leading Matron and the nurses out of the gates and down the track to the gap in the bushes.

'Stay here,' she commanded. 'Nurse Juliet, make sure he doesn't move. Nurse Romeo, come with me.'

They followed the path until it ended in the small clearing. It was deserted apart from a gentle snoring noise coming from a pile of soft grass. Matron pushed the grass to one side and there, fast asleep with a peaceful smile on his face, was the little toad.

'Charlie,' said Matron, because that was The Toad's real name before he was changed into an amphibian. 'Time to wake up.'

She turned to Romeo. 'Just fly back and make

sure the Warlock boy is still there. Then you and Juliet take the little horror back to school and don't let him know I've found Charlie. I have a plan.'

She picked the sleeping toad up and slipped him into her apron pocket. Back in her private room, she tucked him up in bed, locked the door and told Professor Throat to call off the search.

Meanwhile, the two nurse crows had flown Orkward back to the Naughty Dungeon and locked

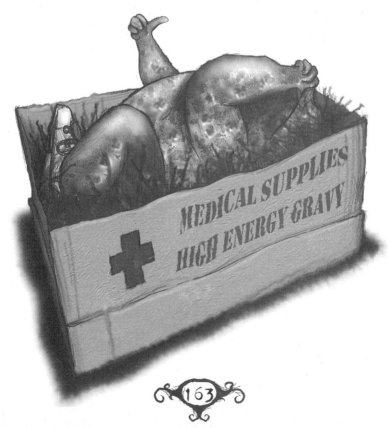

him in there. The Naughty Dungeon was a virtual dungeon in the cellars of Quicklime's that no one had ever managed to escape from, because it was down a very, very long tunnel that led deep into the Earth.[31] It was haunted by horrograms, which are like holograms only very, very frightening. The nicest place in the Naughty Dungeon was inside the toilet bowl with the lid down.

The only thing Orkward Warlock had been better at than any other child in Quicklime's was being locked up in the Naughty Dungeon. He had been there seventeen times and was almost beginning to like it. He loved watching horror movies, and horrograms were like the best horror movies, except they leapt out and slapped you in the face when

---

[31] *The cellars beneath Quicklime College are even more extensive than the ones beneath the Floods' houses at 11 and 13 Acacia Avenue. There is a rumour that the two sets of cellars are somehow joined together even though they are on opposite sides of the planet. There is a more incredible rumour that Quicklime's cellars actually spread out like a fine cobweb beneath the entire planet. This is completely ridiculous and completely true.*

you were least expecting it. He watched them as he crouched in the toilet bowl with the lid resting on his head, but the horrograms still got him.

'That evil boy is up to something,' said Matron. 'We need a mole to find out what.'

'Well, we don't have a mole,' said Professor Throat. 'We only have a toad.'

'Well, what about if we got a mole and disguised it as a toad?'

'Hmm. Go on …'

'I think you'll agree that little Charlie has been a toad long enough, so I suggest we change him back into a little boy and hide him somewhere for the rest of the term,' said Matron. 'Then we disguise someone else as The Toad so he can find out what Orkward is up to.'

'Excellent idea,' said Professor Throat. 'Do you have someone in mind?'

'I do.'

When The Toad was safely hidden away, Matron sent Orkward back to his room, where the pretend toad was waiting for him. Orkward Warlock never looked closely at anyone except himself, and the mole that Matron had disguised as The Toad fooled him completely.

'Where did you get to?' he asked.

'I just fell asleep in the dark forest,' said The Faketoad.

'What about Matron's Enchanted Wax?'

'I left it outside the sick bay door. Nothing to worry about. No one saw me.'

'Excellent,' said Orkward. 'Maybe you're not such a little cretin as I though you were.'

The Faketoad beamed with happiness just like the real Toad would have done.

'And look,' Orkward continued. 'I even conned that idiot Winchflat into lending me his tracking device. We'll go back to the forest and fix it onto Narled. By the end of term we'll be incredibly rich and all the Floods will be dead.'

'You're a genius,' said The Faketoad.

'It'll end in tears,' said The Mirror, who could tell instantly that The Faketoad was not the real Toad, but hadn't the slightest intention of telling Orkward.

The Mirror had seen Orkward in tears more than anyone else had. The whole school knew Orkward Warlock was a sneaky little coward, but only The Mirror knew just how big a baby he was. The boy was even scared of his own shadow.[32]

As soon as it was dark, Orkward and The Faketoad crept out of school and back to the path into the dark forest. The Faketoad was worried that Narled might be able to see that he wasn't the real Toad and give him away, but he was counting on the fact that Narled and his family liked the real Toad and hated Orkward.

Orkward collected his hidden jar of Enchanted Wax, went into the clearing and waited. Soon Narled appeared. He was alone and, as Orkward polished his leathery suitcase skin with his left hand, he fixed the tracking device to Narled's straps with his right.

'Now,' said Orkward, 'here is the package I want you to take to the Floods on Saturday. They'll win the three-legged race. They always do, the cheating

---

[32] *If you had a shadow that kept creeping up behind you and hitting the back of your head, you'd be scared too.*

warthog bottom bristles. When they're getting their gold medals for the three-legged race, leave the package under the winner's stand. You don't actually have to give it to them. Understood?'

Narled zipped the package away and nodded slightly.

As Orkward left the clearing, he deliberately by accident dropped a large gold coin on the path and, sure enough, Narled trundled over and picked it up before vanishing back into the dark forest.

Back in his room, Orkward Warlock turned on the tracking device base station and looked at the screen. There it was, the little blue dot that told him exactly where Narled was. The blue dot came back out of the dark forest and moved further up the valley along the road that passed the school.

'Come on, let's go!' Orkward said to The Faketoad. 'He's on his way to the treasure store, I know he is!'

They waited until they saw Narled pass by the school and then followed him at a safe distance so he wouldn't sense they were there. Eventually the

blue light stopped moving and, as they rounded a corner, they saw Narled standing completely still in the middle of the track. Suddenly he darted between two rocks – but Orkward saw him and followed.

'I've been up this road dozens of times,' he whispered to The Faketoad. 'I wonder why I've never seen this path before.'

The rocks slid together behind them, cutting off their escape.

'*That's* why,' said The Faketoad. 'Now we're trapped.'

'We'll worry about that later,' said Orkward. 'Come on.'

The path went back into the dark forest, getting narrower and steeper until Orkward was almost mountain climbing. The rocks were far too steep for The Faketoad's little legs. Maybe if he had been the real toad he could've hopped up, but The Faketoad was scared he might fall backwards.

'I think I'll just wait here,' he said, but Orkward was too far ahead to hear and besides, he had no intention of sharing the treasure with The Toad.

171

I wonder how Narled got up there, The Faketoad thought to himself.

Orkward came out above the trees and continued to climb. There was no sign of Narled, but he knew he was on the right track. Higher and higher he climbed until at last he reached a wide ledge at the foot of a sheer cliff. Far below him he could see the thick green blanket of the dark forest, and right in its centre was Quicklime College. Behind him was a cave, not just any cave, but Narled's secret treasure cave.

Orkward squeezed through the narrow opening and almost fainted. The cave was massive and, although the entrance was no bigger than half a doorway, the whole place was filled with light. It danced and sparkled in a million reflections as it revealed shelf after shelf of priceless gold and diamonds, and there was more – much, much more. Wherever Orkward

Warlock looked there was treasure, enough to make him the richest person in the world, richer than Aubergine Wealth, and no one knew it was there.

No one except The Toad and Narled.

So they would both have to die.

Orkward scrambled down the path to where he had last seen The Toad, but he was no longer there. He ran back to the two rocks by the road, climbed over them and raced back to the school.

'Seen The Toad anywhere?' he said as casually as he could to anyone he passed, but no one had.

Of course, the real Toad was not The Toad any more. He was now back as himself, a small boy called Charlie, and he was safely hidden away in Matron's own apartment, eating cake and wondering how much lemonade he would have to drink before he finally got the taste of flies out of his mouth.

The Faketoad was not a fake toad any more either. The Faketoad was Satanella Flood once more, and was sitting in Professor Throat's office reporting everything that had happened.

'It was brilliant,' she said, running round in

circles chasing her tail. 'The stupid boy never saw through my disguise for a moment, though I nearly gave myself away when I tried to sniff an interesting lamppost and fell over.'

'You've done very well, my dear,' said the Professor. 'Here, have a gold star.'

'He's going to try to kill us all,' she growled, finally catching her tail and biting it. 'Oww,' she added. 'That makes your eyes water.'

'Don't worry, my dear,' said Professor Throat. 'Narled has everything under control.'

As it began to get dark, Orkward gave up his search for The Toad. He took a backpack of food and a sleeping bag and hurried back up the mountain to the cave. He felt nervous being away from all that treasure, and from the ledge he could see right down into the sports field. He would stay there until the Floods were dead the next day, and then take the treasure and leave the wretched valley forever. He

knew Professor Throat's spell stopped him leaving, but he figured with a big bag of gold, he'd be able to bribe one of the dragons to smuggle him out. Even if Narled or The Toad did give him away, he would be far away.

He was just about to zip up the sleeping bag to go to sleep, when he realised that there was a better use for it. He spent the rest of the night feverishly gathering up the most valuable items from the cave into the bag, until it was bulging at the seams.

Sports Day

The school car park – which wasn't actually a car park because there were no cars parked there – was packed. Every single Blackhound dragon bus on the planet was there. Even ancient dragons had been brought out of retirement to bring all the parents, brothers and sisters and grannies to Quicklime College for sports day. Alzhammer, the oldest dragon of all, had been fitted with a pacemaker and bottled gas, and even then he'd had to set out two months earlier than anyone else to get there on time.

The stadium was packed too. Mordonna and Nerlin Flood sat in the stands beaming with pride. Betty Flood sat between them, thinking that maybe

life would be more fun at Quicklime College than it was at Sunnyview Primary School. It was something she would have to discuss with her parents.

Mordonna's mother, Queen Scratchrot, had been dug up from the back garden for her annual treat. Since the previous year most of her remaining eye had rotted away, but she didn't mind. Leaving her coffin and going out for the day was excitement enough. As the day wore on, the Queen would begin to dissolve into a puddle beneath her seat and have to be put into a glass jar, where she kept tapping on the lid and shouting because she couldn't hear what was going on, though this was probably more due to

the fact that her ears had fallen off than because she was inside a jam jar.

The opening ceremony was, as always, spectacular. The children marched round the field singing the school song which, unlike the anthem, is sung at full volume.[33] When they reached the first chorus, seven hundred white doves were released into the air. Fabulous black clouds gathered over the school. Thunder roared and seven hundred bolts of lightning in perfect synchronisation fried the doves to a crisp. The delicious smell of roast pigeon that filled the air made everyone really hungry and the school cafeteria sold thousands of dollars worth of hot chips, Deadwood Dogs, and the deep-fried mini-gristles that are the droppings of the ballworm.

At Professor Throat's invitation, Mordonna Flood walked out into the middle of the field and held up her arms. All the fathers in the audience instantly sat up straighter and began shouting, 'Take them off! Take

---

[33] *See the back of the book for a few verses of the school song.*

them off,'[34] and all their wives began hitting them with their programmes. Ten more bolts of lightning flew down from the clouds and touched Mordonna's fingertips before racing round the stadium giving everyone an electric shock – something that wizards and witches enjoy in the same way ordinary people enjoy sherry.

'Let the games begin,' Mordonna cried, and as she did so the stadium gates opened and the first competitor from last year's ultra-ultra-seriously-long-distance marathon ran into the stadium. His arms raised high in the air, the winner, Fleetwood Flood (second cousin), did a final lap of the stadium and collapsed at Mordonna's feet.

In the three hundred and sixty-five days since the race had begun, Fleetwood had covered eighteen galaxies and six parallel universes. He had run, swum, cycled, tangoed, teleported and flown through wind and rain, night and day and Belgium. He'd had nine

---

[34] *Meaning Mordonna's sunglasses, because as everyone knows, one glance into Mordonna's eyes and you fall madly in love with her.*

total body transplants, been married twice and even learnt to ask for a cup of tea in Belgian.

As he was lowered into the winner's coffin, Mordonna placed the gold medal round his neck and the spectators cheered.[35]

Mordonna went back to her seat and the field and track events began.

Traditionally the relay race was the first event. Witches and wizards could never understand why people would want to run round a track handing each other a stick, so they changed the rules slightly. Quicklime's relay was much more exciting. Instead of a stick they used a poisonous snake and the point of the race was not to take the snake from someone else but to do your best *not* to take it. The winner was the team with the least number of dead members. The Floods always won this event because of their highly developed team techniques. No equipment or special clothing was allowed, such as barbecue tongs

---

[35] *It would be three days before the second place competitor reached the stadium and by then everyone would have gone home and it was the school holidays.*

or leather gloves, but there was nothing to stop you using your own natural gifts. So Merlinmary always led their team out and simply electrocuted the snake. As it was against the rules to kill the snakes, Satanella then grabbed the dead animal from Merlinmary and ran round the track shaking it violently in her teeth so everyone thought it was still alive. The twins then followed, using the snake as a skipping rope, before Winchflat slipped it one of his special iSnakezombie pills that made it kind of appear to be still alive just long enough for him to carry it past the finish line.

In fact, the Floods won every event apart from the gymnastic dancing, where you jump around on a big mat waving a stick with a ribbon on the end. They found it impossible to compete in that without collapsing in laughter. And they *never* competed in the high diving because, like all sensible people, they didn't do drugs.

Finally, it was time for the day's most popular event: the three-legged race.

The Floods tossed a coin to see who would leave their legs behind and then they tied themselves

together with Merlinmary sitting on Winchflat's shoulders and Satanella jammed in between the twins.

Unlike the other single runners, who had grown an extra leg for the day, Howard Tiny had had himself photocopied. He had lain sideways on the photocopier so only one of his legs got copied.

'You should do this more often, seventy-two, seventy-three, seventy-four,' said Howard's photocopy. 'With two heads we could count bigger numbers, ninety-eight.'

'Yes, and there'd always be one of us

The Three-Legged race attracts many strange entries

there to pull the sock out of the other's mouth, one hundred and one, two, three, four!' said the original Howard. 'I'll ask Mum if you can stay.'

Radius Leg, the sports master, had never been present on a single sports day. He had spent more than half his career in traction or intensive care under Matron's watchful eye. This sports day he was still hibernating under a snowdrift. So, as she did every year, Matron had brought her Radius Leg clone out of her spare parts cupboard.[36]

'Three, two, one, BANG!' shouted the Radius Leg clone, and the race began. As always there were several children who had grown their extra legs back to front. They stayed at the starting line going in circles until the runners came round for the second lap and knocked them flying. Howard Tiny, who was really tiny, got about halfway round the track and sat down on the grass.

---

[36] *Matron had clones for every member of staff, including herself. They had not been created using Winchflat's new Special 3D Photocopier, but by an older, much more dangerous system that often produced clones that were nothing like the originals.*

'I've always wanted to count to two hundred and forty-seven,' he said to his photocopy.

'That's my favourite number too,' said the half-Howard.

After seven laps there were only three teams left in the race. The Floods began the final lap with Bypass Noble, who had managed to grow a third leg with a big spring in it, very close behind them. Two laps back, a small figure hidden inside a paper bag ran as fast as his little legs would carry him. It was Charlie – formerly known as The Toad – and the paper bag was to make sure Orkward Warlock wouldn't recognise him. The trouble was, no one had put any eye holes in the paper bag and Charlie kept getting lost. Also, the extra leg Matron had lent him from her spare parts cupboard was the wrong size and he kept tripping over it. He finished fifteen minutes after the other two teams, but still got the bronze medal.

Orkward sat on a rock outside the treasure cave and looked down into the stadium far below him. Even from this far away he could hear the sounds coming from the crowd. They were sounds that Orkward hated and despised, the sounds of people having a good time and being happy.

He would teach them.

He would give them a new sound, the sound of five revolting Floods children exploding into a billion little pieces that even Matron wouldn't be able to reassemble. As he watched, Narled trundled across the grass towards the medal winners' podium. The Floods, as Orkward had predicted, had won the three-legged race and were standing there looking

disgustingly happy, waiting to get their billionth gold medals. As Satanella ran round the stadium doing a lap of honour, the hatred Orkward Warlock felt for the Floods grew so big he felt as if his head would explode. It was bad enough that they won everything, got all the gold stars, had more friends than anyone else, had the most beautiful mother in the entire universe and just looked so horribly pleased with themselves, but now they had made him get a pounding headache too. As Merlinmary held her hands high in the air and the

entire stadium cheered when she sent fabulous bolts of lightning soaring up into the clouds, Orkward felt the veins on his neck throbbing louder and louder like a bass drum. Blood began to trickle down his nose, blood that no longer tasted sweet on his tongue but was as bitter as his soul.

Narled disappeared beneath the stand and re-emerged a few seconds later. Orkward took out a remote control box from his backpack and switched it on. The red light on it started to flash. It throbbed like a heartbeat and Orkward felt his thumb twitch in excitement. His mouth went dry and his own heart began to beat in time with the red button. He felt faint with excitement.

Ten, nine, eight …

Professor Throat walked forward carrying the medals.

Seven, six, five, four …

The Professor reached down and pinned the first medal to Satanella Flood's collar. She wagged her tail with such enthusiasm that she threw herself off the podium.

Three, two …

Orkward pressed the button.

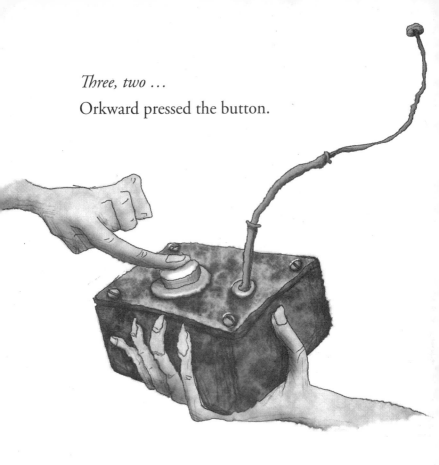

Time seemed to stop. The wind that always ran down the valley stood still. The split second seemed like an hour. The blood on Orkward's tongue, though as bitter as before, now tasted like fine wine, and in that last split second he realised who his true father was.

He, Orkward Warlock, was the devil's child.

He, Orkward Warlock, was son and heir to the dark forces of the underworld and he, Orkward Warlock, would make everyone fall at his feet.

Except then the world exploded.

Orkward was amazed by how loud it was. It sounded as if it was right behind him.

And it was.

The mouth of the cave erupted in an amazing ball of fire. Narled's treasure trove burst out of the cave in all directions. It flattened trees, shattered rocks and blew Orkward Warlock into more pieces than there are grains of sand in the whole world.[37]

Down in the stadium the crowd looked up and, thinking the school had put on a special fireworks display, everyone cheered. Seconds later, hundreds of wonderful things began to rain down on them. Seventy-three iPods, countless gold coins, seven hundred and nine lost buttons, bits of Lego, ballpoint pens, missing pieces of jigsaw puzzles, shoes, and

---

[37] *Not including a seventy-mile beach in north Queensland. If you add that in, then there were fifteen more grains of sand than grains of Orkward Warlock.*

twelve thousand pages of missing homework covered the playing field and half the valley. In the fourth year common room, twelve gold crowns, three French hens and a partridge in a pear sauce flew out of the fireplace as the explosion shot out of the back of the cave and down the secret tunnel Merlinmary had discovered.

'Wow, that was some firework,' said Nerlin Flood as a diamond the size of a chicken's egg landed in his lap.

A small china doll flew through the window into Orkward's old room and landed on the bed.

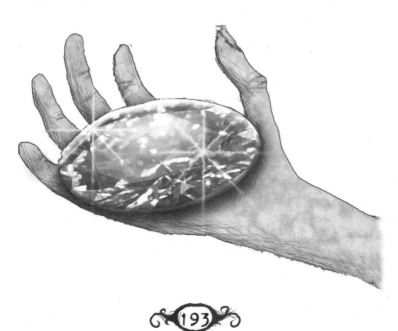

'Beryl, is that, like, you?' said The Mirror.

'No,' said the china doll. 'She got broken years ago.'

'Oh,' said The Mirror sadly.

'Just kidding,' said Beryl, turning back into a seriously gorgeous girl.

'So why haven't I changed back?'

'In a minute, in a minute,' said Beryl, staring at her reflection. 'I just need to fix my hair.'

As daylight went and hid behind the mountains, Professor Throat stood in the centre of the field and brought sports day to a close.

'These have been the greatest games in Quicklime's seven hundred and fifty glorious years,' he said. 'Not just because of the great explosion that showered everyone with gold and diamonds, but because of the great team spirit shown by everyone.'

No one believed him. They all knew the best bit had been the treasure.

'Of course,' the Professor concluded, 'being the seven hundred and fifty-*first* year, a number of great significance in the world of magic, next year's sports day will be even greater …'

Charlie, no longer a toad, was reunited with his parents, who felt so proud of his bronze medal and so incredibly guilty at how badly they had treated him that they spoilt him rotten for the rest of his life. He had a different iPod and Playstation in every room of the house, fourteen stunning girlfriends, a massive plasma TV, his own go-kart racing track and a special secret place in the dark forest where he could visit the little handbags whenever he wanted to.

So that Orkward Warlock wouldn't go down in history as a total failure, a new combined high, low, far and wide jump event was created and Orkward

was awarded a lifetime achievement gold medal as the person who had jumped the highest, the lowest and the furthest all at the same time. But even then, his parents still wouldn't have anything to do with him.[38]

The Floods didn't need a special happy ending, because their lives were just about perfect anyway. Their only worry was being totally unable to think of anything that could make their lives any better.

Back home on the first evening of the school holidays, the whole family sat on the back verandah drinking warm blood slurpies as the ice-cold moon

---

[38] *Come on, Orkward Warlock was vile. He doesn't deserve a happy ending. Anyway, how could his parents have anything to do with him when he was blown up into a million, billion little pieces. Surely that's way too many pieces to ever be put back together again. Or is it?*

And it's not true that Orkward was the devil's son. His dad really was the milkman, and a milkman disguise is much too ordinary for the Prince of Darkness. Or is it?

rose over the trees and sparkled on all the gold medals the children had won.

'I think,' said Mordonna, 'that was the best sports day ever.'

'Absolutely,' everyone agreed. 'At least until next year's.'

Epilogue

'**I**'m not going back to the retirement cave,' said Alzhammer the dragon. 'I mean, what's the point? I'll just get off to sleep again and it'll be time to come here again for next year's sports day.'

'But what about your passengers?' someone asked.

'They're as old as me,' said Alzhammer. 'We'll all stay here.'

Which was how Quicklime College became the first school in history to have classes on false teeth maintenance and how to crochet lumpy things.

The School Song

Oh Quicklime's dark and evil
It is to thee we sing
You fill us full of magic
And help our dreams take wing.

You give us timeless power
And secret ancient curses
You teach us timeless potions
And how to service hearses.

Quicklime's, ancient Quicklime's
Long may your darkness reign
And may you bring the long, long dead
Back to life again.

Oh Quicklime's dark and evil
You turn the day to night
You show us how to sleepwalk
And set our beds alight.

You give us all the magic ways
From centuries gone by
And the secret recipe
For making phoenix pie.

200

```
Quicklime's, ancient Quicklime's
   Long may your darkness rule
And may you bring the long,long dead
   To visit our great school.
```

And so on for thirty-three more verses.*

---

* *Or thirty-five more if you include the two really rude verses that have been banned by the Parents Committee, who know how bad the verses are from singing them when they were at Quicklime's.*

The Weird and Mystical Mobius Strip

Or how to draw on both sides of a piece of paper without taking your pen off the paper.

1 - Take a strip of paper about 20 cm long and 2 cm wide.

2 - Twist it once.

3 - Keep the twist in the paper and tape the two ends together.

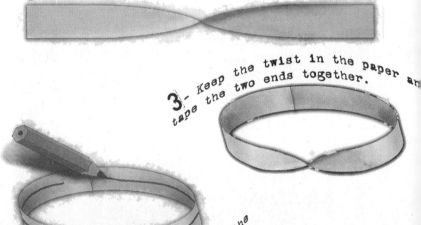

4 - Draw a line along the middle of the paper and don't take the pencil off the paper until you get back to the start.

5 - Try to paint the front and back two different colours.

6 - Cut the strip along the pencil line.

As you can see a Mobius Strip is very weird. This is how Winchflat's friend Eric Ordinaire got trapped inside the internet.

How to Make YOur Very Own
Gristleball

Very few of you will have access to a
giant Patagonian ballworm, so here is an
easy way to make a substitute gristleball
from two simple ingredients.

 You will need:
- 3 million rubber bands
- 2 pints of dragon dribble.

Simply make a huge ball out of the rubber
bands, coating each layer with dragon
dribble as you go. Then leave it in a
festering ditch for a month to ripen.
(If you can't get dragon dribble, you
can use anything that leaks out of your
baby brother or sister.)

The Quicklime College Teachers Files

PROFESSOR THROAT
NB, PDF, PS
HSC(Ghent)

Professor Throat is the fifteenth Throat to hold the job of headmaster at Quicklime's. He has been unable to find or manufacture someone strange enough to want to marry him and so when he retires, he will be the last Throat to run the school. There are plans to dig up his grandfather and put him back in the job.

Matron has been secretly in love with Professor Throat for years, but her love is so secret that even she doesn't know about it.

The Professor is a fair man (except for his left foot, which is actually very dark), and generally loved by one and all.

His best friend is a Belgian Mongoose called Rembrandt, who lives in the dark folds of the Professor's gown and only comes out during a full moon.

PREBENDER GLORIOUS
Invisibility

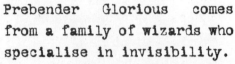

Prebender Glorious comes from a family of wizards who specialise in invisibility.

Because of this brilliant talent, PG's relatives are behind some of the greatest and most daring unsolved crimes in history.

PG himself has a defective gene which makes his invisibility totally unpredictable. It means that he might suddenly appear at a very bad moment. Because of this he has been unable to enjoy the great rewards the rest of his family have earned. The world of crime's loss, however, has been Quicklime College's gain. His lack of control over his own invisibility make his classes very entertaining.

RADIUS LEG
Sport with Pain

Radius Leg was originally built out of
bricks and changed into a PE teacher
with a special spell.

Because of his origins as a building, he has a very high pain threshold,
though not as high as he thinks. During
his teaching career he has followed
a very strict training regimen which
has resulted in the carefully planned
breaking of every single bone in his
body.

DOCTOR MORDANT
Genetic Engineering

Doctor Mordant is, quite literally, a self-made man. Beginning life as a small blob of bacteria growing on a piece of mouldy camembert, Doctor Mordant began the exciting path of evolution when a live electric wire came into contact with the cheese. In a matter of hours, he had grown a few legs. A day later his arms appeared, and by the end of the week he was a fully qualified school teacher.

His evolution continues to this day as he is unable to decide exactly how many legs he would like to end up with, and what colour the broccoli growing out of his spare head should be.

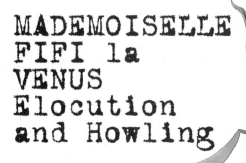

MADEMOISELLE FIFI la VENUS Elocution and Howling

All the male teachers and most of the boys at Quicklime's are in love with Fifi la Venus, and who wouldn't adore her delicate wings and armour-piercing scream?

She's the only person to have shattered every single window in the Sydney Opera House while singing in Moscow. At night she roosts on a nest of phoenix feathers in a special tree in the school quadrangle.

MATRON

Matron was built out of concrete in the same factory as Radius Leg and spent the first fifteen years of her life as a shed full of lawnmowers on the edge of Quicklime's playing fields.

Her two nurses, Romeo and Juliet, lived in a nest inside her roof until one night, during the greatest storm of the century, they were struck by an incredible bolt of lightning which actually had nothing to do with the storm but was caused by Romeo eating through a power cable.

This coincided with the old Matron *actually* being struck by lightning so Matron and her two nurses were given the job.

Over the years since then Matron has invented and collected an awesome and scary dispensary of spells and medicines.

MISS PHYLLIS
Special Breeds

Miss Phyllis has the unique distinction of being the only person to have both won a top award (Best in Breed - Cuddly Pet Class) at Cruft's famous dog show and been a judge in the same show.

The Special Breeds children adore her. Not just because she is a kind, caring person, or because she can cook seventeen amazing dinners out of nothing more than a rat, two sheep's ears and a tin of dog food,* and not because she never makes them learn boring things like Maths and Belgian, but because she is absolutely brilliant at catching a red rubber ball in mid-air.

---

* *You might have actually seen Miss Phyllis on her famous TV show* The Mouth-Watering Mongrel.

211

AUBERGINE WEALTH
Economics and Other
Forms of Burglary

Starting with a mere five million dollars given to him by his grandfather on his fifth birthday, by using his natural talents, Aubergine is now worth more than Belgium and Italy added together.

He enjoys the finer things in life, such as expensive wines, platinum wands and Gucci broomsticks. He dines on corn-fed endangered species and even the gravy stains on his dicky* come from Harrods and were made by a top chef.

He teaches at Quicklime's because as an ex-student he wants to give something back.

---

* Don't be rude. A dicky is a false shirt front worn to keep your shirt clean. Like a posh bib for grown-ups.

THE OTHER TEACHERS

There are a lot more teachers at Quicklime College and other staff, like Narled and Doorlock, who keep the school running smoothly. Unfortunately we don't have enough time or space to meet such wonderful people as Arkforth Prenderfoot, who teaches dead languages (for dead students), or Geraldine Saltwater, who teaches Underwater French, or Diabolus Prawn, the Underwater Dancing teacher, who is only part-time because the rest of the time he is a bookcase.

Maybe in a future book we will return to Quicklime's and meet the legendary Lord Algernon Tuppence-Change, who teaches sinew weaving, and Sugar-Cane Molasses, the world famous tango dancer.

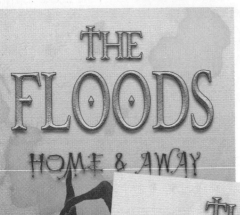
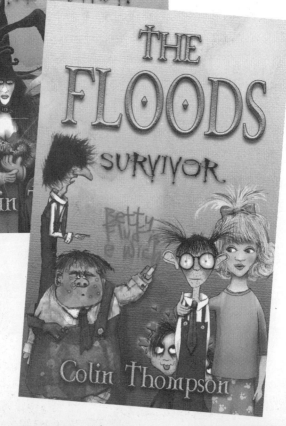